KINGS
OF
BIDONVILLE

Republic of Folium—Rays of Dusty Glass

PATRICK C. JEAN-PIERRE

WESTBOW
PRESS®
A DIVISION OF THOMAS NELSON
& ZONDERVAN

WestBow Press books may be ordered through booksellers or by contacting:

WestBow Press
A Division of Thomas Nelson & Zondervan
1663 Liberty Drive
Bloomington, IN 47403
www.westbowpress.com
1 (866) 928-1240

ISBN: 978-1-6642-0045-6 (sc)
ISBN: 978-1-6642-0044-9 (hc)
ISBN: 978-1-6642-0046-3 (e)

Library of Congress Control Number: 2020913995

Print information available on the last page.

WestBow Press rev. date: 8/24/2020

CONTENTS

ACKNOWLEDGMENTS

Some of us explore this world through the eyes of Folium, the proverbial wondering bee who climbs out from her hive, circles around, and then declares there is no God. Trapped by the wrinkles of time, the truth remains hidden to her until she decides to spread her wings and become free.

Thank you to my supportive wife and creative children for bearing with my imagination and members of my family for entertaining the concept of this book. This work is made possible by God's grace and favor.

INTRODUCTION

Two young men, Raymond—the seventh generation of Rimon the patriarch—and Dan of Nile, estranged descendants from two districts of Folium, set out on a spiritual quest. Bonded by a secret pledge to free their people, they fled by way of the besieged town of Bidonville to Mosaic Point, Africa, where their forefathers once sojourned in search of the liberation of their enslaved people. To atone for their nation's disobedience and broken covenant with the Most High, their fathers traveled to a Jewish temple and received a revelation. What lies ahead is the fate of their people. They must choose between two paths: liberation if they fulfill the commission or the Sisyphus curse if they fail.

It is revealed to them that the commission had not been fulfilled, hence Folium's cycle of depredation. Raymond and Dan would come to be Folium's last hope, but they must first discover this in their own personal quest. Their journey would lead the newly acquainted men through the depths of two worlds. United by a binding promise, they were unaware of the hidden secret that was capable of destroying them or earning them rights as kings of Bidonville.

CHAPTER
ONE

•••

Africa: Patriarch Quest

They are dying again, a slow and cunningly silent death, and they don't even know it. It's unclear if dancing this final dance with fate will conjure life or an evolved state of isolation surrounded by hidden enemies of their fathers. Like little bits of broken glass passing through their entrails, their demons are poised to remain dormant killers until their appointed time. A fleeting glance into their past, however, where the parallel between literal autonomy and spiritual authority remains distinctly clear, reveals their destiny as free men and women, but a question remains. Will they rise to become a liberated people or remain nationless slaves of Folium?

While erasing certain time-tested truths from their history, Folium diluted their faith and deleted their identity and origin, conniving them into abandoning their essence and chasing vanity and trivial things instead. The assimilated people of the growing empire run through the broken fields of an inescapable maze, searching in darkness for knowledge, birthing in their carnal institutions, meaningless pleasures in a cyclical manner— from darkness to renaissance to the return of darkness. Among them are the distinguished gents of the aristocracy, groomed and inducted into the bestial system, living their days in a dense haze as sub-phased kings who would become pawns designated to days of misguided and futile rulership. These once-prominent men transitioned into multilateral kings hold siege on their people over and over again with unfortunate consequences.

As members and druids of secret cabals and organizations with no national loyalty—corrupted by a desire for power and blinded by unadulterated pride—they rule over the unsuspecting people of Folium with unanimity. They undermine the holy faith by changing the names of places and altering the times along with the canons of universal laws. Dominant in the area of the hidden, they captivate the people's essence by employing the mechanism of a well-guarded secret.

The few who suspected the connivance climbed the watchtower to see the light but were eventually pacified to step down to meaningless things. The critical race against time to avert a final death at the hands of an unseen adversary was spearheaded by failed revolutions, but attempts to rearm the casualties have been abandoned throughout the generations. This retreat from what is just emboldened their sovereign rule. The regeneration of past triumphs and tiring defeats have successfully taken hold of Folium's morale, spiraling her into an endless, maddening cycle of doom.

On the home front, fallen soldiers of old have no one left to take up the good fight, leaving the fate of the people in the hands of the awakened few. Idleness and ignorance of their purpose further seal their fate into mindless slaves of a heathenish system that has diverted their captured freethinking minds into meaningless things. Hidden to these many unsuspecting minds is a slippery slope to an elusive future where they will finally agree to give up their souls.

Folium has encountered a final saving grace, however, but it is up to her people to receive it. The thirteen elders of Freeland begin a quest to reveal that truth and liberate the minds of Folium's captives, but they will eventually learn that time is always a factor.

Navigating the Mosaic

It is at the beginning of spring in the six hundredth lunar cycle. A remigration of elders and followers of the faith has begun its genesis in an attempt to preserve their ideologies and cease the depopulation of their indigenous people. They are heading to the east as sojourners fleeing the beastly system of the Republic of Folium for wisdom and spiritual authority. Amongst the group are religious elders, intellectuals, and objectors of the royal house. They are forerunners to the others who would follow at the behest of the Final Call. Traveling on foot and domestic animals to a hidden location by the connecting seas, they carry their personal effects, gifts, religious relics, and a yearning desire for a liberated Folium.

Throughout the night, the *Mosaic* waits under cover of dense fog. Docked several miles away from the populated part of the district, not easily noticeable from the primary and secondary roadways, the ship unobtrusively awaits. Watchmen surrounding the floating wooden whale take turns as lookouts and prepare to offer guards of the royal house explanation for the ship if questioned.

Finally, at dusk, the rest of the men covertly arrive and hurriedly board the large ship. As the anchor recoils, the captain requests that his crew assume their posts. They set the sails and adjust them in the direction of the wind. The crescent moon is barely visible amongst the hugging clouds, but it serves as the first point of navigation. As the night settles, they embark on their voyage with no molestation from the royal guards.

The refreshing blue sea, in its thickness of pure marvel, splashes its salty waves against the long round hull of the slow-moving *Mosaic* as they pass the edges of the divided continent. Rocking and cradling the men on the assurance of past voyages, the sea waits for their command. Several young men of the three hundred serve as guards on the upper deck, and others are manning the sails, positioning them at the captain's direction.

Within hours, the sun rises and paints the sky with soft streaks of apricot yellow on a light blue cotton canvas. It welcomes the ship to the promise of a new day. They have not been met with opposition and take comfort on the successful departure thus far. The mainland is still visible from the forward-facing deck, but no threats are imminent. They repose their vigilance and resume the minor tasks of the boat.

Within moments, coming into view, the heads of eccentric ships ascend the horizon. The larger and more visible of the intimidating fleet blindingly flashes the sunlight, reflecting from its extended metal mast an awesome sight. Its roaring head gorges the rushing wind as it parts the ocean beneath its sharp hull, crossing the *Mosaic*'s course.

"Waves at ninety degrees!" yells the first oarsman of a smaller ship, rowing adjacent to it.

The oarsmen brace themselves as they navigate inland. Untraditional in their garb and in their masts, they command attention and a bit of a panic. Appearing rather royal in their design and purple hue, they terrorize the passengers and the crew. More ships like these begin to appear on the horizon, following in one after another and engaging the incoming waves like swarms of crows at dusk.

The men of the *Mosaic* draw out their nautical scopes to study this parade of the sea, filled with a fearless campaign of Goliath-like men mightily propelling large vessels toward the mainland. The elders and others on the ship react to the incoming ships, taking up defenses because it is not uncommon to encounter pirates in these seas.

"What is the nature of their business in these waters, Captain?"

The passengers continue to study the ships' architecture and peculiar heads. It is as though the dark clouds above these foreign-looking vessels are dimming the very sunlight at the horizon.

"Rest assured, men, that fear of death often proves mortal. The more you hold onto that fear, the more life you give it, birthing an enemy that begins as an imaginative thing. It will gainfully enslave you and ultimately destroy you. Put down your scopes, men, and focus—beyond the ships and crashing waves—on the future that confronts you. The raiders of the mind are among you. It is in plain sight. Do not look upon their sigils with marvel. They are a reflection of the maps of the mind."

A gust of wind enters the motionless waves, rattling the metal rings against the mast and sending a few of the men into panic.

The captain surveys the deck and tries to raise his voice above the sounds of the wind. "The alternative mind they seek to create in you is only possible if you allow it. Do not allow them to build into your mind the reality they seek to create. It is only possible if you open the gates of your mind."

Veering further away from the view of the shoreline and mountain peaks, they question if these strangers are traders of goods or supplanters who would seize their land. They gaze with bewilderment as the spectrum of purple and decorated wood streams by into their national waters.

"This is unfathomable. I dread the thought of what may happen if we are confronted," says one elder as he moves his hand from over his head to his mouth. Not expecting a response, because he intuitively knows the answer, he says, "Captain, you have told us before that these seas have beneath them an array of lay lines cross-sectioned and emitting into our coordinates. Could we be under attack by gods of the sea or—perhaps worse yet—prohibited passage to the *Mosaic*? What do you think?"

At the sound of an enormous whirlpool, evidence of their gushing oars vanishes, along with their foggy impairment. The sails of the *Mosaic* flutter against the rising smoky wind as they move farther into the open sea. The question to the captain remains unanswered, and their imagination stirs with the possible outcome from the encircling fleet.

"I see the luminous waves coming in with the tides, Captain! Shall we rein in the sails and change our direction?" an eager voice shouts.

"No. They are merely passing through. There is no need to fracture the paths to avoid contact with these men," replies the captain.

One of the elders exclaims, "Look straight ahead and avoid making eye contact!"

Whispering to one another, an elder with an Arabic accent replies, "They bring with them mysteries from afar. They are exporting ideologies and customs to our land."

A young man turns and says, "And what do you make of the ideologies?"

The elder takes in a deep breath. "My young brothers, remember what I am telling you. If you want to destroy any nation without war, make adultery or nudity common in the young generation. This will be your sign of what they are exporting to your land."

Another man replies, "Is it not the speculation the fathers once warned us of?"

With his face concealed from the wind, another elder responds, "A king may move a man. A father may claim a son, but even when those who move you be kings or men of power, your soul is in your keeping alone. When you stand before God, you cannot say, 'But I was told by others to do thus. Virtue was not convenient at the time.'"

Suddenly, a large whale emerges from a distance, perhaps fifty yards from the ship, and lets out a large sound.

As the men look in the direction of the massive creature, an opposing wind rattles the sails. A subtle whisper grips their attention, "The raiders are here. The raiders are here. The raiders are here."

In the evening, the twinkling stars and their constellations blanket the night and serve as additional navigation points. From his vantage, the captain monitors the progression of the days and nights to route their path. Figurines of the peaks of waves and flying fish fizzle away from the waving moonlight and blend in with the immensely mysterious sea. The waves become visible on the surface whenever the moon casts her illuminated light and then disappear again. Streaks of her beauty ripple with each raindrop, and they flicker with each passing sparkle. A mirrored image of the changing cloud patterns creates a glazed reflection of the large ship as it streams across the hidden plains, ridges, and basins of the Atlantis. The fantastic voyage of courageous men driven by personal ideologies and collective principles and a desire for change maintains a steady course to Freedom Land.

Stroking his long black beard, elder Rimon approaches the captain and joins him under the silky canvas of the wooded upper deck. A gentle evening rain whirls in the chilly breeze. The draft occasionally rattles a subtle golden bell suspended above the captain's canopy next to a tall ladder dubbed by the crewmen as Jacob's ladder.

The captain says, "Your journey lies beyond the humble shanties of Bidonville and beyond the illustrious man-made mountains of Folium to a place where the wise and brave sojourn. I must ask you, my brother, why must you travel so far to see what is already inside of you?"

Rimon says, "You reason well, oh, Captain, oh, Captain, my, Captain. Your words are true and true, but these conditions are also true. The optics of Folium makes that which is near and that which is far beyond virtually impossible to see. At Mosaic Point, I sincerely believe, that spiritual authority has not lost its sovereignty. Prayers to the Most High and spiritual revelation from him are magnified to those who seek the Light."

"And what is to become of those who cannot see the Light, my good man?" asks the captain.

"As you have taught to many, the truth remains so. If you seek you shall find," replies Rimon.

"And how do you know you have found the Light?" asks the captain.

Rimon, leaning forward, tilts his head to see the sky and raises his hands to the incoming rain tapping against the canopy. "The Light already knows us and will reveal himself to us. The Light is truth and justice. He is love. There is no such thing as distance to the Light. It is immaterial."

The captain smiles and asks, "If the Light is here, why can't you see it where you are?"

Rimon closes his eyes and softly replies, "Because I must first climb out of the darkness. There, with our brothers, we shall seek the face of the Most High to reveal to us what is hidden to our natural eyes and the amazing grace we have forgotten. With this illumination, we will free our people and the rest of Folium."

The captain turns over the back of his hand and asks, "And what if Mosaic Point were to exist here in Bidonville or anywhere else in Folium and was not geographically limited but created wherever *His* people calls upon His name?"

Rimon looks to the sky and replies, "That my, Captain, is the great quest."

A white dove flies over their heads, presumably seeking land, and disappears into the night. Her squawks fade as she vanishes from sight.

Embracing the Mosaic

After months in the Atlantis Ocean, the *Mosaic* finally arrives on the shores of Freeland—welcomed by unmolested flora, birdcalls, and large rocks that push against the surrounding landmass. There, nonthreatening sea creatures bobble about on slippery barges and feed on wild sea mushrooms. The skies are dressed with colorful birds, inserting in and out of the lush green jungle. Healthy truffles hide beneath fallen trees, displaying the richness of the black soil and the splendor of the land's possibilities. The exotic flowers and docile creatures speak to the uniqueness of this foreign land. The obedient gestures of every tree sway with every westerly wind, bringing calm to the atmosphere.

As the men discuss the most appropriate method of deployment, they take in the sights. The *Mosaic* towers over the shoreline and embraces the water as it toggles between land and ship. Her passengers look down at the sparkly blue waters and inhale her salty mist as fish swim closely by.

The crew is ordered to create two lines of exit. One is for cargo, animals, and materials. On the other end, parallel to the other exit ramp, is one for the men. As the first rams descend, the passengers start to disembark. Drawing a sword to point to the distant mountain, a crewman shouts, "Gentlemen, this is God country. Look at her majestic mountains and ocean rimming around her gracious fruit trees and waterfalls. She is our link to the time-consuming quest to Freeland."

"Captain, how many nights do we have before us?" asks an elder as he replaces his head garb. Some of the younger men step ashore with their sheathed swords above their heads.

"This is going to be a long night of cutting through this thick green jungle. The tree barks are wet and slippery," another replies with miry fingers and a preoccupied mind.

The captain places his compass in his side pocket and answers, "Judging by the phase of the moon, we are a few days away from Shabbat." Calibrating his nautical scopes, he calculates their location. "Hmm. We are at the back of the Promise River. If I trace our path from this point, it leads our course through the Desert of Grace and eventually a rest at the kingdom gates. We can dispense our camels and loads there to replenish for the long trek. If we regulate our pattern between rests, we should arrive in a few days. The trail is long, but it will lead us there eventually." He points to distant mountains. "On the other side of those peaks are vast deserts that lead us to our destination. We can replenish our water supply at the rocky waterfalls there. The trail is arduous. It will be more favorable there for our animals since the plains will level out. This first step in our path, as strenuous as it might seem, will take us to Mosaic Point if we stay the course."

An elder holds his knotted water gourds. "We have sufficient water to get us to the passage points and watchmen at night." He crouches down to pet a dog he calls Sirius and tosses a stick into the water. "I calculate we can hold out for a couple of days without incident." He holds his broad belt.

The captain says, "Yes, there is a reservoir beyond that stop where we can drink again and refresh our horses and camels."

A crewman leads the other animals off the *Mosaic* and onto the passive shore. Each man mounts his personal effects on the side bags and trails inland. "Many wise men have walked these beaches before us in search of the same answers to an age-old conundrum. Who is Folium—and what is her purpose in the grand scheme of things?" Stroking his long beard, he inquires, "Do we not see her for what she is?" He pauses to study their expressions. "Look at this shell in my hand, gentlemen. What do you see? Can you appreciate its inner spiral?"

The man standing closest to the shell says, "We see a mere shell, Elder."

The captain looks upon the elders standing around Rimon and smiles.

Rimon says, "A scholar once argued that there is a mathematical equation to all of creation. I agree with this argument. Creation is not a nebulous concept left to man's interpretation or mere happenstance. Creation is divine. Could we claim that Folium is as her name implies—a mathematical equation? Is Folium divine? Has she lost has luster, unlike this pearly shell in my hand? Has man corrupted the original intent and purpose?"

A sage on a decorated horse taps his servant on the arm and points to another seashell on the ground between two porous stones. "Go and bring me that rock."

Rimon responds, "No, my good men. You are looking at more than a rock. Look closer—and you will see."

All the men, but for the elders, stare into the smooth inner shell, but they cannot see what Rimon is revealing.

Rimon says, "Some will see a cyclone, others a flower, others a golden rule, and others nothing more than a rock. But in this clever clue, we can observe the path to Folium. We do not see or know where her spiral ends. Seek, and you will see my fellow brothers. Seek, and you shall find. Seek, and you shall see. At last, the legacy of this conundrum endures."

The group set up a temporary camp for a few days and nights under towering palm trees. The stay is longer than anticipated. Their flickering fire is concealed by the hugging ironwood trees and the overgrown green flora. On the seventh morning, they head for the distant mountains onto the harsh, yet often completely hydrated deserts of the Sahara.

The familiar morning breaks into the eastern Saharan sky with anticipation as it bears the sprawling apricot sunlight on the faces of sleeping camels and shifting sand dunes, yielding their sharp curves and edges to the whirling sub-Saharan wind. The gentle wind twirls from the southern regions, finagling between the silky valleys and troughs and inscribing lines and patterns throughout. They sculpt an endless field of patterns, each with distinction and likeness of a forgiving sand papyrus.

Over the sand ridges, footprints from the night before disappear with new patterns formed by the brisk morning wind. The menacing wind whispers as a child's tender song and inscribes the patterns of the new day. The vast desert widens to a brilliant sky filled with birds traveling eastbound with fresh olive branches in their beaks. Watermarks give way to the early dawn, remaining camouflaged to the desert's golden possibilities.

A partially hidden tiny bell beneath the hot desert sand slowly disappears with each passing desert gale. Hidden gems remain concealed from the sojourners traveling with their band of high-humped camels, which are strapped with commercial goods and personal effects. Some hold preserved religious relics and artifacts in carefully wrapped boxes. Others carry nothing more than anticipation.

The sun is unforgiving, and its pounding heat menaces the travelers as they try shielding their sweaty brows to catch a glimpse of the path before them.

The afternoon sun is at its pinnacle, evaporating every ounce of vigor in their step, but they are determined to reach the temple before the eleventh hour.

Rimon encourages the men, saying "May God hear our prayer and deliver our people. We must stay the course, follow our accepted devotion, and find the way."

When they are 1,201 miles from Mosaic Point, sparkles of sunlight pierce dusty glass jars of precious clear and amber oils. Precious gems rest against other gifts, secured tightly by velvet wrappings. Their shadows no longer precede them. They follow the humps of the camels, reach another milestone, and narrow the span of their travel. The band of camels pauses to replenish from the afternoon's stinging heat, assigning their load on the palms trees dotted throughout a water hole and emerging from a narrow ravine.

Wrinkled hands of an elder penetrate drizzling water pouring from an alabaster vase. One of the elders, Goshen, reaches in his sack, draws out a long wooden flute, and begins to play devotedly. The simple instrument plays along with the motion of the desert's flowers as they collect trickles of water from the elder's gourd. He squints toward the grand temple afar, barely visible from the shimmering mirage and gusty sand, and then he plays a melody of healing and meditation. Casually removing his dry lips from the flute, he wets them again and says, "What the kings may know is very, very little compared to what God has revealed to the wise." He continues to play. The music echoes in the ravine below, inspiring the small birds to sing along. The song of praise fades upward as the men draw closer with their eyes shut and arms open wide. The wind brushes against the camels' reins, elaborate wooden saddles, and brass mountings. The melody seems to stop time, effacing the memory of the laborious travel and conjuring a spring of inspiration. The elders and the other individuals begin to pray to the Most High.

As with each passing hour, the travelers continue their migration, approaching the temple. With each interval of dispensation, they stop and pray. For days, they repeat the cycle. After crossing a low valley, they set up a new tent. For three days, they rest on the banks of the Promise River.

Rimon bends down on one knee, interrupts the serenity of the river with several ripples, and glides his fingers on the smooth surface. "The Most High has seen the condition and cries of our people who are living in Folium and will deliver them in his time. May he find us worthy to break the chains of our bondage."

CHAPTER
TWO

•••

The Temple:
Shabbat

On the seventh day, the men from the *Mosaic*—sojourners of Folium—arrive at the temple in time for Shabbat. At the lead, Rimon the Patriarch, with a tightly wrapped sachet to his waist, reins the camels for passage through the needle, the village's main entrance.

As the procession of three hundred men enters the city, they face the north and praise the Most High for a safe arrival. Revealing a box strapped to his horse, Nebo, Rimon presents it before the temple's guards for inspection. In it is a tasseled scroll with a message for the head rabbi. It holds the Prayer of Councils and a detailed plea from several elders from the Folium Empire. As they enter the temple's captivating halls, they remove their head coverings in subjecting to their custom, which forbids men from wearing a head covering during prayer.

In the temple, a call to prayer echoes through the ram's horn. A bowing rabbi commences a melodious chant into an age-old scroll, occasionally looking upward as acolytes follow along. The impressive temple, not too distant from the cascading dunes and scattered camels, welcomes many indigenous and transient tribes for Shabbat prayer. Their shades are as diverse as the colorful walls they stand against, filled with rhythmic and melodic echoes and poetically setting the atmosphere as they enter the center hall.

During the annual pilgrimages, council members representing various nations address the congregation in their native tongues. In response, the leading rabbi and other members of the council enunciate from the sacred book of prayers, from the canonized *Book of Wisdom and Salvation.*

In his native Aramaic tongue, the head rabbi begins by reciting the holy psalms. The custom is non-tribal and egalitarian, though it is rooted in the sacred canon that has survived Folium's evolutions. "In the words of the Magnificent, the Most High God, we greet you in peace."

The elders repeat the ceremonial opening in the language of every sojourner present.

Addressing the travelers from the Upper Rhine, another councilman, a rabbi reads Psalm 91: "Celui qui demeure sous l'abri du Très Haut Repose à l'ombre du Tout Puissant. Je dis à l'Éternel: Mon refuge et ma forteresse, Mon Dieu en qui je me confie!"

From all who are present, throughout the corners of the world, a response is given before the Holy Scrolls: "Amen!" The Egyptian origin of the word *Amun* is effectively applied in its Hebrew redefinition to affirm agreement.

The rabbi keeps his face bowed before the text.

Others respond, "Amen!" They begin to sing, extending their sounds for moments on end. The harmonious octet is on a frequency that turns their minds to prayer.

As the lexical diversity development continues, an Ethiopian elder gestures for the Amharic version of the prayer.

Another speaks in Arabic, saying, "Whoever dwells in the shelter of the Most High will rest in the shadow of the Almighty. I will say of the Lord: He is my refuge and my fortress, my God, in whom I trust. Surely he will save you from the fowler's snare and from the deadly pestilence. He will cover you with his feathers, and under his wings, you will find refuge. His faithfulness will be your shield and rampart. You will not fear the terror of night, the arrow that flies by day, the pestilence that stalks in the darkness, or the plague that destroys at midday. A thousand may fall at your side, ten thousand at your right hand, but it will not come near you.

"You will only observe with your eyes and see the punishment of the wicked. If you say, 'The Lord is my refuge,' and you make the Most High your dwelling, no harm will overtake you. No disaster will come near your tent. He will command his angels to guard you in all your ways. They will lift you up in their hands so that you will not strike your foot against a stone. You will tread on the lion and the cobra. You will trample the great lion and the serpent.

"'Because he loves me,' says the Lord, 'I will rescue him. I will protect him. He acknowledges my name. He will call on me, and I will answer him. I will be with him in trouble. I will deliver him and honor him. With long life, I will satisfy him and show him my salvation.'"

The consecrated ceremony continues into the late hours. The men slowly stand up from their prayer rugs and retire to their sleeping quarters. Some remain in the halls longer than others. The appetite for holy fellowship is serving them well. They reclaim victories over their homelands, rebuke curses, and break the strongholds on their people by binding the evil entering from the north, the south, the east, and the west of Folium in the name of the Father, the Son, and the Holy Spirit.

In the morning, as the rising sun pierces the windowless openings in the ambient glowing room, men move about and greet one another. Others admire the indoor fountains, inanimate sculptures, and symbolic gifts presented to the council. Inside the worship hall, the withered candles from the night before morph into stubs of wax inside golden cups, and the incense diminishes into soft lines of ash. The scrolls remain open on the final text read to the room of worshipers and sojourners.

Across the intersecting halls, laughter and discussion mingle with the clattering of white-adorned plates and silver utensils. Fresh figs, plump grapes, and hot tea decorate the fasting table. Several guests take their seats. Small groups pass in the halls with warm greetings as they pause to study and admire a painting displayed as the *Wilderness of Sinai*. Others returning from the outside garden begin to break their fasting by taking in offered pastries.

Rimon and the other twelve elders return from the Rephidim library to meet with the thirty-three priests of the temple. Rimon calls on an esteemed delegate and asks in Hebrew to see the head rabbi. "My good man, Shalom, Aleichem."

The representative replies, "Aleikhem, Shalom."

Rimon says, "May I have a word with the head rabbi before he leaves for his chamber? My men and I have an important matter to discuss with the council. I understand that they are meeting shortly this afternoon, but I wanted a moment of their time before then. We have traveled far and trust the head rabbi can appreciate this."

The delegate leads the men into the grand round-table room with oversized doors. "Gentlemen, you may enter here. The high priest has been informed and will see you momentarily."

Upon their arrival, a suspicious character leaves the room they are about to enter. He pauses briefly and looks over his shoulder at Rimon and his twelve followers. The suspicious character keeps a firm grip on scrolls pressed firmly to his chest. His elegant robe strapped with a sash and royal claw pendant impresses upon Rimon that the summoned documents are from the royal house and have been sent by the king. With a puzzled look, Rimon begins to wonder if greater things are at play. Before he can inspect further, he is hindered by the beckoning delegate.

The thick mahogany doors open to a large cyclonic table with enrobed men sitting around it. "Your Excellences, I present to you Rimon and the twelve traveling followers from the four districts of Folium."

"Rabbi, Rabbi, in honor we come before you," says Rimon.

The head rabbi gestures for Rimon and his men to sit. "In respect, we receive you."

Rimon says, "I am Rimon from the lineage of Freeland. My men and I have traveled far from the westernmost point of Folium on a pilgrimage in the last hope to save our people from what has been a gripping curse on the followers of the divine laws. They are prisoners to an emerging empire that firmly plants its feet on the backs of its people. Many have rebelled and sought refuge, but others continue to live under her tyranny. As their spiritual leader, we must defend them. We took an oath many years ago to protect the innocent and observe our duty to our God and nation. We, therefore, ask for an intercession and blessings from your kingdom, great council."

Outside of the temple, the camels grow restless as the desert sand shifts beneath them. The disturbance soon becomes a swirling monsoon, which overtakes those mounting their beasts of burden, forcing them to quickly secure what they can and retreat to the entry halls. A servant unravels the veil tucked into his turban, shields his face, jumps onto a horse, and races away to follow his master. They disappear into the haze of stinging brown sand. The horse's neigh fades behind the royal tents, and others call to their men to do the same.

"Rimon of Freeland, we know who you are. We welcome you home, our brothers, victors of the depopulated indigenous nations of Folium and the wanderers of Continuum. I bless you, and on behalf of this council, we support you in your endeavor. Your people are in multitude and have traits that many in your new land mistakenly consider different tribes. While we are one global family under the Most High, we recognize you, Rimon, as a descendent of tribes of the High Priests. We know, and they know, your true origin and purpose. I will go into who *they* are in a moment, but I must first advise you of a critical element that you must take to task to ensure the validity of your travels. Your people and the many of the quasi-republic must relinquish all intangibles of captivity to seek this higher understanding. They must refuse to submit to offenses toward the Most High and atone for their transgressions. They are a lost people of no nation, nomads in a land artificially created to function as farms. They migrate here and there for sustenance or presumed freedom, but they are still captive on this same proverbial farm. They cannot see it for what it is because they have been put under a curse and been lulled into accepting their prison as described to them. Shall we go farther?"

"Yes, honorable rabbi," replies Rimon.

"Allow us to share with you, men of Freeland, part of a long-concealed secret," says the rabbi.

Another rabbi says, "Many have come here for tenets to new and reforming religions and some for favor of this council, but we refused them because their hearts were full of evil. Their motives were self-serving."

A third elder says, "There are larger matters at play that you do not yet understand—and we must reveal them to you. It concerns the souls of your people and the pledges they will make with every precious child born under the royal seal."

The head rabbi says, "Beware, for even the very air they breathe will belong to the royal house and the Council of the Exiled High Priests. Verily I tell you this, babes of the sea are upon you. Each child in Folium in effect is stock, bonded by the Crown, which when released by his mother, is like the seas releasing her traveling ship from a forty-week voyage to the royal docks. They are consequently tantamount to the property of the royal house. It doesn't settle there, my noblemen. These new arrivers into Folium are subject to new laws, man-made laws. Folium proceeds to rewrite the laws written in their genesis code to alter their essence. This agenda signifies a level we cannot delve into now, but it is critical that you note it for our discussion. There is a fleeting time race to hold claim over these ships and their destiny—for amongst them are kings and queens of Folium." Holding onto a long staff, he points to a large book. "We call them, in the language of the south, Inkosis. You must reclaim and possess that right before our adversaries do, lest you again coalesce your energies into another folio cycle. You must prevail sooner than later, or the Folium matrix that is devising around you even now will swallow your people into another paradigm."

"And who are our real adversaries?" asks Rimon.

The head rabbi replies, "You will know them by their roots. Look closer, and you will see they are supplanting the hearts of your people."

Rimon asks, "And what do we make of these roots? How will we identify or distinguish the difference between our adversaries and advocates?"

"Do not be deceived by one of their greatest deceptions. They have already manipulated times and places and the physical appearances of the nations. Similarly, they will try to change the universal laws and mask them with man-made laws. Do not look on the outer surface or appearances or what you hear from the mouth of man. Look at the essence of the people. We are, after all, souls living hidden to ourselves in dying vessels. We come to know who we truly are and our divine purpose once we find the source, which is the Most High God. This quest perhaps is the greatest catalyst to the convergence of the *Mosaic*. All of Folium—and even the rest of Continuum—will look at your shaded faces, say you are not a Hebrew, and hold that against you. They will say you are from this tribe or that tribe and do not have a legitimate ground to free the diasporas. Do they know the lineage of your mother? The landscape of roots will become murky throughout the times. This confusion will lead to the smearing of your history from the chronicles and sacred traditions. Do not let this dissuade you. This is part of the deception, the master plan to subvert the people, all the people regardless of their ethnicity. The scheme will thrive right before your eyes, silently and invisibly, with subtle clues that will escape the imagination of many. Why is this piece of information important? The Most High is not a respecter of persons, none more valuable than another, but there is an element to your roots that ties back to covenantal authority. As elders, you must teach the people their true identities in the Most High, revealed to us by the great Messiah. Do this wholeheartedly, lest they be fooled again into accepting the one assigned to them and subjected to the curse spoken upon their destinies. I will reiterate to you again, men of Freeland, teach the people to know themselves and the unknown name written in *The Book of Life*. Teach them to know that an inherent power lives in them that will become the prize in the end. They must never allow it to be altered or transcended by Folium and rulers from the invisible kingdoms who seek to control and eventually destroy humanity." The head rabbi points up with one finger and holds onto his robe.

Distress develops on the faces of the thirteen. One of the councilmen points to his temple and says, "Rimon, we have not forgotten those we appointed as woodcutters and water carriers for this assembly. Their cunning ruse saved them on that day because they understood the principles of the Most High. There will again come men who will approach you in the same manner, but beware. These people are very different from those your fathers knew. They will come before you with mixed intentions. They are pagans, masters of the air, land, and seas who quest to subjugate foreign and domestic lands.

"They will collaborate with your kings and sages, showing the people great marvels that will subdue your land, their liberty, and their very souls. When the eyes of the people finally begin to open, the adversaries will close them again by placing in front of the people creations of their hands, meaningless things concocted from other worlds. They are masters of many tongues and sciences, which they will use in their favor, crafting skillful treaties and laws that even the elected will accept. After the golden moon will come the silver moon, and at that eleventh hour, time will reveal it to you. You will see their true nature and attempts to supplant the current order with a beastly order. As gatekeepers, you must charge strangers to your camp with a task—one they will be unable to refuse. If they fail, you will know them for who they are because their fruits will bear witness of their roots."

The mahogany doors remain closed for hours as the gathering continues. On the other side of the door, muffled voices penetrate as the guards continue to defend their post. At the end of the final hour, the head rabbi says, "Men, stand and make yourself heard before these witnesses of the assembly. Take this oath … if you accept."

The noblemen place their right hands on their chests. "In the name of the Most High, we renounce the Folium curse and the darkening patterns it brings."

A councilman says, "The enemy you battle against cannot be seen with your natural eyes. Don't underestimate this mighty foe. The enemy's powers have had no limits, and his authority has continued to grow with each passing age. It is not a physical battle you fight or a new one. We have been at war with these adversaries for centuries. They have found a kink in our armor. Therefore, your methods should evolve and not remain as they were in the past."

They hand Rimon and the other elders each a large book with words that describe the liberation of Folium.

The leading rabbi folds his aged hands, closes his eyes, and says, "All who are here have seen, and all have also heard, it is forbidden to cross this sacred seal of life with a third. We so swear to uphold this oath. Thank you. Our gratitude is immense great elders of Mosaic Point."

The men conceal their faces and return to their camels. The royal delegate is nowhere to be found, but Rimon discovers a clue left behind—perhaps it was part of the document he carried in with him. *He returned to his tent and had not left the compound at all. He dropped these papers as bait.* Rimon studies the cryptic pages. "Lord, the giver to the wise, give me the understanding to interpret the mystery language in these pages," Rimon prays quietly. As he concludes his prayer, he overhears a conversation between two men who appear to be savants.

"You say that language is a pattern?" one philosopher asks.

"Yes, that is my well-documented hypothesis in Kemet from where the Greek gain their knowledge."

"If that which you say of semantics be true, then we can argue that language is a key. I would reason further to say that creation is subject to a unique language. Since mathematics is a language, we can conclude that the universe is one enormous mathematical equation. Would you not agree?"

Rimon focuses on the encrypted document in his hands. He soon realizes that he is looking at a map of the universe depicted as a mosaic of stars. The map points to the mathematical interpretation of Continuum's structure. "As go the stars, so goes Continuum," Rimon whispers. "The king is trying to alter our physical reality and must be at a loss of the primordial laws to fulfill his agenda." He gasps for air, tries to control his breathing, and whispers, "A world absent of a life force to make the way of an anti-Folium." Rimon runs to his horse and joins the other men.

The animals surprisingly endured the assaulting monsoon without incident. Rimon, mounting his horse, exclaims, "We have before us, men, a monumental task, which will determine Folium's tomorrow." Raising the sacred book in the air, he shouts, "This is the sword of the Spirit we carry with us! It is the fiery sword capable of dividing the soul and the spirit! Who here among us bears this sword?"

The men reply, "We do—and we are with you, brother!"

The Fiery Sword

Bringing their humbling stay to a close, months after their long voyage, they meet in their modest tent for a final night.

Rimon says, "Men, put on your armor. A great battle awaits us in Folium. It is greater than what we have seen with our naked eyes and is raging furiously against the people of Folium as they sleep. We are now aware of what we have before us, and we are keen on the principles of the kingdoms and its dogmas. This sinister realm we fight against is not from our world—and neither are its powers. That world and our world intersect at critical points. We must formulate our plan very carefully. Although we have the backing of the council, if the royal house finds us out, do not reveal what you have learned here today. You are to guard the sacred sword with your life. You are to defend the seal with your sword and swear allegiance to the Most High God to the very end. Are you with me, men of Folium, sons of the Freeland, soldiers of the Most High God?"

The men respond, "Yes, brother! We are with you! We will preserve the sword, the sacred text of the Most High, and the honor of our bond."

Rimon asks, "Are you against the kingdom of darkness and its hidden cohort—or are you with the kingdom of the Most High?"

The men respond, "From the kingdom of the Most High, we receive this sword. To that kingdom, we will return. We will defend the innocent and submit ourselves to the sacred seal in this holy book. Folium! Folium! Folium! We have reclaimed the victory!"

Racing camels and horses pound the courtyard, ushering the declaration for the new Folium.

CHAPTER
THREE

•••

The Folium Condition

C hasing the indefinable concept of the Infinity, Rimon, the twelve, and the three hundred bearers of the faith left behind a metropolis of human inventions of towering monuments of greatness where bliss begins and culminates in the creative imagination of their carnal minds. They are returning to their land with a renewed purpose. Their adopted homeland, renowned for its evolved civilization, finds itself contending with a great curse. Its people, consisting of many tribes and tongues, are gripped in the trenches of dissonance—trapped between carnality and an unyielding desire for more power.

Ensnared in wrinkles of time, Folium toils in vain to build what is, what once was, and what will soon cease to be, remembering not the former generations. Not even those yet to be born will be remembered by those who will come afterward. Myopic in their outlook and bound by linear and cyclical limitations of time—the past, present, and future—they are unable to see. The idea of it is quite daunting. Spiraling into inevitability, the cycle of time has repeated itself in Folium. With it has come about a universally suppressed truth, remaining unveiled to those who could look to the Infinite Light for meaning, but hidden to the myopic, the unconscious masses and the babes amongst men. This hidden world will become Reimonde's Folium to discover, the seventh generation of Rimon the Patriarch.

The opulent Republic of Folium sits on a splitting gap between the seams of righteousness and lawlessness, widening with each generation to greater extents. She is gripped in the wedges of her own devices, unable to free herself from the slippery quagmire she created. The metaphorical gap that began as a small surgical fracture courses through the foundation of its fifty-foot walls, government courts, sprawling villages and towns like a sprouting vine making its way from the core of her materialism and ungodliness.

Overflowing onto the gleaming pillars of her regions and beneath the bedrock of the national cathedral and other sacred sites, it widens secretly and silently, spreading indiscriminately between poor and wealthy towns, circuitously maneuvering from the east to the west.

The crack is now a deep chasm, traveling far from the deserts of Freeland and Mosaic Point into the heart of the Republic of Folium. Its seismic shift continues into the years, silently coursing into the base of the squares, where the revolution would inevitably begin.

As sojourners of Folium, Rimon, and the elders began their exodus from the four districts with these conditions at heart. Recognizing the pattern of the times, these spiritually orientated spectators in a land that has seen the progression, suppression, and regression in an almost cyclical evolution began their quest, drawing closer to the Infinite Light which is, and which was, and which is to come, the Most High.

Through the intercession of the council and empowered by the sacred seal, they begin the unearthing of the corrupted empire and liberation of a captive people. Upon their arrival, they established the Order of Magma, valiant men who pledge to the decree of the Most High, rising to disarrange the order of prophetic visions of the king's men. Members of the Magma embed themselves in different segments of society, protecting the virtues of their creed in every capacity. They built the university to uphold the divine decree of the Most High and instruct spiritual soldiers from amongst the youth. From the illustrious branching of their membership, they birthed objectors of the social order, objectors who secretly work to ignite the great revolution. They created the university in a succinct discipline to instruct, liberate, and empower his people for the invisible wars and battles of the mind.

King's Clothes and Exiled Priests

Standing motionless in front of a glaring mirror, a newly appointed king of Folium extends his arms laterally toward his faithful attendants as they dress him for the Great Summit, a consortium of the kingdoms. His attention soon gives way to his recollection of the previous event, the recent Summit of Sages held in the seven hills of Folium's religious district.

"Your excellence, lend me your ears if you please," pleads a hunch-backed man and his kneeling wife, both presenting themselves humbly before the king as messengers of a faraway kingdom. They resemble the same hideous likeness and stature of the images in the books of the False Sages. "We have traveled many miles with this urgent message from the lords of the royal societies. There is a war among the families over who will take claim of the next harvest. As landholders of this planet, they look upon Folium and are not pleased by the unfolding of the agenda. They ask that you accelerate what has been outlined, for the sun of this sphere will descend upon Continuum, consequently leaving their baskets empty. Will you do them the justice of filling their baskets, the scales of their harvest, your excellence?"

In frustration, the king replies, "I am but one man operating against the matriarch, and I cannot broker the fruits of Folium with the limited range given to me. I only control one-fourth of a world, while the family of pantheons has full reign to control many worlds, including Continuum. The relics of yesterday do not work any longer. The people are becoming wiser and are keenly aware of the twelve cycles. The methods are looping through but rendering different results. We are experiencing a renaissance out of this dark age, and for this, my kingdom is asunder."

The female companion replies, "Your Excellency, do not become aggravated. You are a wise king who understand the times and seasons. Our lords have made arrangements for you. It has been written on the walls of your courts and delivered in the writings you have read to your stools. The legal means have been given to you to respond accordingly and cultivate the fruits of Folium in the entire sphere of Continuum. Our lords ask a minor contribution in return, a little collateral, wise King."

His brief flashback is interrupted by a knock at the door, and the voice of his groom of the stool asks, "Your Excellence, the priest has arrived.

Shall I entertain him in the courts—or shall I assign him to the clerks or the clergy?"

The king's daughter approaches the servant. "Yes, of course, in the courts … because the king is wearing nothing at all at the moment. Tell him that the Excellence is completing some final affairs and will be with him momentarily. Father, I have already ordered the bearers to open the gates."

"Very well, my child. I am deciding on new garments that the two travelers, the light carriers, advised me to wear. They say it will help me decipher the priest's position and wit when he arrives." The king adjusts his curly white wig beneath his ordinated crown, a distinction that is unfitting for the clothes he foolishly believes are supernaturally endowed.

Unbeknownst to the populace, a diabolical plan was at play to circumvent the autonomy of the districts. A manifesto is delivered by the priest to the king's court, drafted by the Council of the Exiled Priest and guarded by the royal knights. The stool unravels the declaration for the king's seal of approval. It contains a detailed plan on how he is to transform Folium systematically in a way that even the most watchful will not be able to discover. The king intends to officiate the ruling at the eve of the great harvest where many of the chosen few would attend from throughout Folium and from abroad. Inside the closed chambers of the king's court, parts of the manifesto are revealed by the king's men.

Beneath the red seal of the Council of the Exiled Priest reads: "I hereby take claim over the *personas*, which by divine institution and universal power of the king."

One of the king's council members leans over to him and whispers, "Every pledge will belong to you, my king."

The king grins and replies, "And to whoever serves the council."

A Magma spy, observing the whole unraveling from the guise of a servant, retreats to the semicircular tower above a loaded ballista where a messenger waits for his cue. He arrived the night before under cover of night and disguised himself as a pauper traveling from the Boucherville district. After hearing the awe-striking revelation, he retreats to his camp on foot, crossing over the Bile River to where his horse awaits. He wrings his soaked robe, places it in his black and brown sack, and rides into the Ephraim forest on the outskirts of the district.

Standing up from the roundtable, Rimon leads his men into prayer, calling unto the heavens, for the manifestation of the Most High. "Great omnipotent and omnipresent Father, we humbly come before you. We ask that your Spirit descends upon us. Through the Spirit of the holy and sanctified Yahushua Hamashiach, we call upon your name." He continues with the prescribed prayer at length.

One of the elders leans over to Rimon and whispers into his ear. He shares news delivered with the guardsman's timely arrival on an unsaddled horse.

Rimon motions for his entry.

The guardsman, returning as a spy, removes his hood and greets the elders unrobed and with wet undergarments. "I have just returned from the far district and have seen with my own eyes what they are preparing. They are planning, my brothers." His chest swells up and down as he tries to control his breathing. "They are organizing. They are conspiring to do something to the people." He gasps for more air. "I rushed over the mountains away from the towers with my horse. My horse was exhausted. I was exhausted, but I moved quickly. I made haste and climbed that mountain. Eventually, I reached the port and met a delegate at the gate who granted me passage out as you said he would. What they are doing is diabolical. Quickly! Quickly! You must hasten and tell the other brothers. You must tell them what the king is plotting. You must alert the people."

An elder says, "This cannot be. How will they manage to coordinate such a great move in such a small window of time? Isn't the harvest about to commence in a few months?"

The guardsman replies, "You will understand after I tell you this. In their midst, the Great Lady of the remote districts commenced the meeting. She arrived in many ships, which are regarded as her children. The woman came in ship number one and returned to the seas. She returned again in ship number two and left for the harbor. Within the same hour, she returned to the third ship and retreated to the harbor again. She did this twenty or twenty-seven times in that one single time. Finally, as she stood on the balcony to address the delegates, a large boom was heard outside. I immediately thought it was an attack on the ships. Many ran with the others to see what the matter was. I could not leave. I was disguised as a table servant and did not want to compromise my cover. I remained inside with the others, but I asked a doctor to explain what was happening outside. He shrugged while observing from his vantage point on a lounge. He would not reveal why this was happening and why in the world the Great Lady would arrive and leave again and then return so many times in one day. This procedure did not make any sense to me. He had no answers for me and would not clarify what I was witnessing.

"I looked up and saw the ashes rising high in the darkening sky. To my amazement, the twenty or twenty-seven ships sank completely in the harbor. As everyone lamented, including her poor eunuchs, I changed into my robe and left the mansion, never looking back. I soon realized that the woman was symbolizing something terrific. I discovered the meaning of this masquerade. As I left the room, I recalled the names labeled on the ships. They are the names of the nations she bore in a single day, conceived as a woman in labor, in close succession, but on that same day, just as they birthed, they all perished the same day, all had fallen to their deaths. They were stricken by a massive mountain from the sky, causing a dramatic and fantastic death that no one could prevent. After witnessing this striking image and receiving this revelation, I stood there motionless and stunned. I ran to the kitchen and escaped through the back door, where the gourds and alabaster vases were stored. I nearly broke one in my escape, but I managed to escape without drawing attention. From there, I headed for the Bile."

Rimon, surveying the men in the room, says, "Brothers of Freeland, while this revelation transcends the understanding of the simple, we must proceed in our resolve to warn the people. These developments must not and cannot overtake our resolve. The wicked king, at this very hour, is subverting our spiritual safeguards and may soon ransack our critical positions and ancient boundary stones. We must not delay a moment longer."

The third elder grips the edges of his breastplate. "The moment has come, gentlemen."

The call to action brilliantly fills the room with justification for a moral response, a counter move to the king's agenda.

Rimon thanks the Most High, blesses the room, and says, "May the Most High God be with us!"

Many days later, with the help of the order, word of the king's plans finds its way to the masses like a wildfire raging down a mountain. It is silent to the unwise and sleeping members of Folium. For others, however, it agitates civility and shakes the status quo that kept them docile for many years. Throughout the districts people say, "The babes are upon us!"

Like the erupting heat of magma, Folium's silent revolution begins.

CHAPTER
FOUR

•••

Out of Many Came One

I n Slogtown, a band of men joining as one mind arrives at the royal printing
press to meet with the aging overseer. Each is carrying oil lamps and standing
in front of the cold iron gates. They peer between the decorated black bars
to obtain the watchman's attention. Ringing the suspending golden bell, the
leader of the lamp carriers says, "May we please speak to the overseer? We have
a request sent to us from members of the lower district that we must present
before the wise one of this district. Will this house accept our appearance?"

On the watchman's person are twelve sacks affixed to his belt, each
containing magnesium, calcium, and potassium, the essential salts of
the human body. He raises one of the sacks above his shoulder and asks,
"Young man, you are the salt of the earth, but if the salt loses its saltiness,
how can it be made salty again?"

Amos replies, "Sand, salt, and a mass of iron is easier to bear than a
man without understanding."

The watchman asks, "And to whom do you hold your allegiance?"

Amos responds, "In the beginning was the Word, and the Word was
with God, and the Word was God. My allegiance is unto the Most High,
the author and finisher of my faith. The beginning and the end. The alpha
and the omega. He is my salvation."

The guard raises his staff and allows Amos to enter, but the other seven men are told to wait outside and not extinguish their lamps. Amos is led through a long hallway dressed with luxurious rugs and literary publications from the upper districts and illustrations of things that have yet to be rediscovered and reinvented in Folium. These portraits of the royal house and Council of the Exiled Priest stuns Amos, and he carefully follows the watchman. The eyes in the pictures seem to follow him as he walks toward the overseer's chamber.

The overseer is standing between two large paintings. Amos sees a sun on a cross and a fisherman leading twelve men across a sea of stars.

"To what do I owe this visit tonight?" asks the overseer.

Amos quickly replies, "Were you expecting someone else, sir?"

"No." The overseer tightens his lips, pauses to reflect, and replies, "Well, my correspondence led me to believe that a Greek gentleman would arrive with an urgent request. Your elders must have altered the commission. I suppose they sent you instead, young man. Very well."

Amos smiles, concentrates on the paintings, and looks at the overseer. "Looks can be deceiving, sir. It all depends on what you are looking for." Unraveling the tassel from the coarse papers, Amos clears his throat. "We have a proposition for you that we hope you will accept."

The overseer moves his gray hair aside, takes his seat, and rests his arms in the large armchair. "Have a seat young man."

Amos takes a seat and replies, "Thank you. Allow me to begin with the first order of business." Amos reaches into his coat pocket and hands the overseer a small purple sack filled with sparkling diamonds. "I can assure you, sir, that these are not blood diamonds."

The overseer smiles and gestures to Amos with his outstretched pointer finger. "You are a few centuries before your time. Sit here instead. My assistant is rearranging the library. You will be more comfortable here. Would you like something to drink—perhaps something rich and light?" The overseer reaches for a dusty glass table cluttered with three small glasses and an opaque bottle of strong drink.

Amos replies, "No, thank you. I am a man of a sober mind ... if you understand?"

Leaning to his left to place the sack in his desk drawer, he says, "Indeed ... a man's gift makes room for him."

Amos nods, leans forward, and places his documents on the desk. He points to specific areas of the document and begins to describe its content and what he wants the overseer to publish in the almanacs. "Are you aware of the Seal?"

"Yes, of course. It has been under fire lately."

"Yes, the sacred book is under attack, but so are the people who openly profess it as their creed. What we have learned of late is that there is a modified copy circulating about Folium that is abundant with debauchery ... perhaps to dupe the people into forsaking the original covenants." Amos folds his hands on his crossed legs. "It seems lately that the fleeting sanctification of our creed is seen by many at a faint distance. It is dimmed in conversation, obscured in dogmatic correctness, and nearly extinguished in the face of all global creeds. The learned men in Folium, who have been in this sphere for but a moment, think of themselves as enlightened and thoroughly learned of the matter of this universe and dilute freedom and beliefs, resolving them as dispensable and therefore nonchalantly ignore assaults on faith. The average man sadly knows not the difference. Tattered by a constant volley of ignorance, the omission of God on official parchment is leading him to relive history's abysmal past."

"And what makes you say this?" the overseer asks. "Do you think that this house is responsible?"

"No, sir," replies Amos.

"Do you intend to publish a correct and upright copy in my publications?" asks the overseer.

"Not entirely." Amos uncrosses his legs and leans closer to the overseer. "What strikes me as strange is that whoever is circulating this copy is doing so in an unusual pattern. We believe that they are diluting important words and omitting elements that tie back to the original covenant. Ultimately, the plan is to create confusion and alter the people's consciousness to see good as evil and evil as the whole of the law. To further control them, they are causing the masses to curse themselves with their mouths and the members of their bodies. I have seen agents and human beings memorialized and praised in the middle of the square as representatives of the holy kingdom. Folium misguidedly proclaims them as kings. I believe we are living under a great curse that is reversible, but we need your cooperation."

"And you intend to reverse the curse with words? What an optimistically bold target you pursue. Let me share with you a word of wisdom." The overseer removes a quail feather pen from his robe pocket and gently places it on a pile of books on his desk. "There are many books written by wise men that say otherwise, but I will quote from *The Book of Wisdom and Salvation*: 'The fear of the Lord is the beginning of wisdom, and knowledge of the Holy One is understanding.' If they do not hear it, how else will they know who to fear? They are ripe for harvest, Amos, but the question you must ask yourself is this: For whom will they be harvested? Go and find the covenant between the people and their God, and you will find the key to breaking the curse. In the name of Christ, you will have that authority, and through the covenant, you will be set free."

Amos replies, "We know this to be the truth, oh wise one, and we have climbed the mountains of the *Mosaic* for this revelation, but this is only the primary aspect that we have inspected. The more difficult part—the less visible piece—is the reprogramming of their bio-seal, the sacred helix. We understand the powers and effects of words, images, and their vibration—all in all the same to the essence of Folium. This is the element of their affliction we seek to contend with."

The overseer replies, "Vibration. You have said a great deal and appear to have obtained much understanding. I don't say this lightly when I tell you that we are moving into a new age, which will make your work even more challenging. Darkness is upon us and has agents working against you and your people day and night. You are holding in your hands a balance between life and death." The overseer dips the quail feather in an ink fountain, writes a note, and hands it to Amos. "The predictions of the Most High are written all around us—as a reminder of his greatness and his promise. As you said earlier, it depends on what you are looking for. Why cast your pearls to the sightless? Why not focus on those who are among the knowing, Amos."

Amos replies, "While we are not the Light, we bear witness to him who is the Light. Through us, the Light is shown. Therefore, I don't have that option. I am a light, a servant of the Infinite Light."

The overseer replies, "Hmmm ... well said. Well said. Funding is not the same as it once was. Whoever this is that you speak of, they must have a very high-level connection and deep coffers. Do you understand that the population as a whole will not believe this notion we have discussed today? You have to maintain your approach very delicately."

Amos replies, "Of course, which is why I am proposing that you submit the messages in this next cycle of your publication right before the next harvest."

The overseer says, "Excuse me for a moment. I have to take this."

An assistant peers into the partly lit room. Amos stares at the magnificent paintings. The one displaying Pleiades and Orion catches his attention.

The assistant says, "Yes, sir. I understand. No, sir. You will not have to do that, sir. He will arrive in the morning."

Fiddling with his fingers, the overseer replies, "Tell the others to see me in fifteen minutes." The overseer turns to Amos. "Okay. Where were we? Amos, you have your orders, and I have mine. Your strategy remains a delicate line we walk on. We have to be very careful."

"I agree," says Amos. "You must assure me that your publications will arrive at the foot of the hills before the harvest. It is there we will see more impact. They will reach the masses from there. The masses are under greater oppression and are more desperate for a revolution. That is the strategy."

"Yes. That will not be a problem."

After shaking hands, the overseer removes his thin-framed glasses and points to a distant garden outside of his window, which has several points emitting from its center. "What you see there, my nobleman, is our principal patron and financier." A long lounge chair carefully positioned near the large window briefly takes Amos's attention for a moment. Compelling images of war are tightly woven into the embroiled tapestry. Above it, A-E-I-O-U is prominently displayed. He focuses outside the window to follow and whispers to himself.

"What's that, Amos? Did I hear you say something? Did you say *release the stronghold*?"

"I am sorry, sir. Continue, please," replies Amos.

"You have to contend with them. I, therefore, can only promise a few subtle publications. You do not want to raise suspicion. You are on your own from here," says the overseer.

Amos replies, "Very well. We shall resume again next week."

The seven men outside notice Amos and elevate their lights to receive him at the gates.

"Gentlemen, the brothers of the House of Amos, judgment is coming, and those who have ears and can hear the written words shall run to the towers of the Most High and shall be saved," says Amos.

Aeolis says, "Brother, and what of the overseer?"

"The overseer agrees to publish the messages, receiving payment on one hand, but he must prove to us if he uses the other in kind," replies Amos.

The first of many publications prints the following week. In it are cryptic messages for the central districts to be conveyed to the weekly gatherings at the cathedral steps in the lower regions.

Many months later, the publications serve their purpose and begin to make a significant impact. The daily conversations of the masses begin to change in the right direction. More people are waking up to the king's deceptive agenda, the actual reasons behind the newly passed laws, erected images, and insistent creation of meaningless things. The king initially presented them to the people as a primrose path to greatness, but it later revealed itself as a ruse to legitimize an emerging pagan empire.

The almanacs are one of a series of methods of communication to reach the sleeping populace. As segments begin to wake up, one district at a time, their focus shifts from meaningless things to the heated matter at play. Those having this new consciousness are finding higher ground in their new understanding. In their enlightenment, they see what they could not have seen before. Their eyes are now open to an accelerated slide toward the edges of an approaching cliff. This conundrum, its consequences, and a siege under a tyrannical empire are evident to the masses as never before.

CHAPTER
FIVE

...

The Harvest

A multitude of rapidly shuffling feet worriedly cut through the beaten paths of the hills, under the boroughs of a heavily laden forest and the cover of night. The protected points have provided the perfect shield to the underground passage points. To avert spies from the royal courts, they form secret phrases from the sacred book. The guardians' advisors to members of the Magma and guides to the fleeing group hold strategic positions in the crossings. The men of the order reestablish their positions and remain concealed throughout and above the mountains. Anyone entreating entry must answer a consecrated challenge to the members of the Magma: "Out of the mouth of babes and suckling hast thou ordained strength because of thine enemies." The one requesting passage has to respond correctly. If the response does not correspond, the members lead them to an incorrect path—and sentinels seize them. The mountains are steep and unwelcoming to those taken as captives.

An eagle and vulture gawk at the barely visible sums of people inconspicuously crossing over the territorial border. Men, women, and children endure this rite of passage for their safety with hopes that they will arrive at the gathering place before the next harvest. Across the border, between the valleys, they assemble. They appear at another point where more guardians await, ready to challenge them again. The guardians are responsible for engaging anyone who responds to the questions incorrectly.

They are the gatekeepers, authenticators of the gathering place. In their hands is the sacred *Book of Wisdom and Salvation* provided to them from Freeland, which now guides the sojourners out of Folium and to the hidden mountains.

Three elders stand at the entrance of a narrow path and unveil their heads to reveal themselves to the first group in line.

"What is the nature of your visit?"

The men in the group look at each other and to the elders. "We seek refuge, sirs. What we must we do to be saved?"

The elder responds, "Do you believe in The Most High and accept him as your Lord?"

The travelers answer, "Yes. Yes, we believe and accept the Most High."

Raising his arm to pull the golden bell, the elder responds, "You and your household may enter."

The small groups travel throughout the night, passing boulders scattered on the backs of the hidden mountains, bridging one plane to another. Like rocks floating on top of a deep blue ocean, the stones serve as a reference point for each group. The passage points continue to direct those with a new consciousness, the sojourners, away from the squares of Roulerville, the wealthy and middle class, Slogtown, the working class, Bidonville the serf/agricultural class, and Boucherville, the slave class. The four geographic pillars of Folium are the spiritual pillars of the empire.

Before dusk, on the opposite side of the meeting mountain, restless crowds forage far below. They encircle Folium Square for the harvest. Like children enjoying the pleasures of meaningless things, they partake in the festivities. Celebrated members of Folium entertain with song, and chatter electrifies the afternoon.

The king approaches the royal tower. "May I have your attention?" He looks upon the people and smiles. "My beloved sons and daughters of Folium, I have something to share with you at this hour. It is of utmost importance. I request your attention. As you know, your king loves you and takes careful steps to protect you against those who seek to do you harm. My goal is to ensure your safety and happiness. Last night, spies were captured. They had been collaborating with the enemy. My brave knights discovered them working with external enemies in the eastern regions. You have nothing to fear, nevertheless. The crown has it under control. They have been captured and will be brought to justice. Because your king loves you, I decided to allow the festivities to continue, but I must leave you now to address this matter. My people, what say you?"

The people reply, "Long live the king!"

The king asks, "What say you?"

They reply, "Long live the king!"

Again the king asks, "What say you?"

They reply, "Long live the king!"

The king asks, "What must we preserve?"

The people shout, "Folium, Folium, Folium!"

As the foolishness grows with their shouts, an image of the king is revealed before them. The celebration continues for hours. Later, the king's men request that the children appear before the tower to receive delicacies. One by one, they run for their positions in line. They stand before a large brasslike grimace of a thing and stare upward for their promise.

The night beams up as the king's men light up the base of the tower. Folium's sweltering furnace welcomes the selected youth of Folium with brilliance and flair. It has arms that stretch out, extending beyond its beastly form, like a wolf receiving his prey. Members of the royal house place piles of red apples on each hand as parents dance around the statue with their children. Its golden form glows and illuminates the faces of those standing close enough to feel its heat. Some of the older boys are given insignias, welcomed as proud members of the Royal Junior Corps, and instructed to raise their right arms to salute the image. They chant the royal song.

Entertainers dressed as royal guards inundate the streets, parading throughout, forming rings, and giving out candy and other hard delicacies. Waving at the children, they chant, "Long live Folium."

Other representations of the conveyed message continue throughout the night.

"Long live Folium!"

"Long live Folium!"

"Long live Folium!"

Harvest Wages

At the turn of the century, the antics remain the same. Folium has kept its promise as a long-lasting empire and has managed to suppress the overt revolution. The kingship governs under a new name. Power remains in the hands of the elite dignitaries. Governing bodies remain under the same coverture—but under new names and a new coat of arms. Folium exercises its authority under ministries, including the ministries of justice, agriculture, and truth.

At the twelve hundredth harvest, the festivities are relatively eventful. The masses are appreciative of this annual event, and the gathering provides an opportunity for fellowship, jesting, drinking, and pure merriment. The beastly furnace of antiquity, which once received red apples, has been replaced by towering buildings surrounded by manicured mushrooms. Attendants greet children as they enter its creatively carved doors. They cheerfully give out desserts and miniature statues that resemble the beastly furnace.

In other parts of the square, the air is filled with fermented fruit and—in some sections—a healthy stock of horse manure and burning charcoal. At the fountain, close to the baker's table, children chase one another and enjoy baked delicacies. Their parents sit nearby, sipping on hot beverages and discussing the social events of the day. As the amusement continues and attention to detail starts to dwindle, fireworks are set off, demonstrating marvelous luminosities in the sky.

Later in the evening, an announcer approaches the podium near the garden's fountain. It is the prime officiate of the ministries of justice. Two young men with black umbrellas shield him from the light evening shower.

He announces, "My beloved sons and daughters of Folium, I have something to share with you at this hour. It is of utmost importance. I beg of you for your attention."

The music stops playing, and the chatter quiets down.

"Your government loves you, and it takes meticulous steps to protect you and ensure your happiness. But, as of late, we have learned of terrible events that we must bring to your attention. It saddens me to say that your safety is at stake." He is careful not to utter the word *freedom* because the word would support some sense of personal entitlement and autonomy. The people of Folium have been conditioned to believe that freedom is a privilege of the collective, not the individual. The state would not want this impediment in its coveted quest for ultimate dominance.

"Last night, spies were captured collaborating with the enemy. We discovered them working with external enemies in the eastern regions, nearly bringing down the very fabric of this land we all cherish and love. Listen to me well, my beloved, when I tell you this: our love for you is unyielding, and we will do whatever it takes to protect you."

The crowd is stricken with blinding love. They raise their hands and chant, "Folium, Folium, Folium!"

The prime officiate asks, "My people, what say you?"

The people reply, "Long live the state!"

"When one of our own betrays our land, we must do the only righteous thing, the only reasonable thing, to preserve this union between the state and its beloved. The conspirators have long attempted an assassination on members of the ministries, but now we have claimed the triumph. Therefore, for your safety and the safety of this body, I now declare a temporary cessation of the charters. Through the recognizance gathered by the royal courts and the Folium ministries, we accumulated a list of names. These yet-to-be-identified individuals will be pursued, captured, tried before you, and terminated at the brook."

The crowd cheers. "Down with the enemy of the people. Down with the enemy of the state. Down with the enemy of Folium!"

The prime officiate asks, "What say you, my people?"

They reply, "Long live the state!"

Again the prime officiate asks, "What say you?"

They reply, "Long live the state!"

The prime officiate asks again, "What must we preserve?"

The people shout, "Folium, Folium, Folium!"

In a little while, when the heightened patriotic zeal had reached its pinnacle, their acquiescence proves to be detrimental to the republic. Weeks following that harvest, one by one, innocent men and women are rounded up and terminated. They came for members of the district objectors, farming class, clergymen, and certain ethnic groups. The royal house accuses them of belonging to the Order of Magma and terminates them ceremonially. No one speaks up, growing more fearful of the paternal head of the ministries and their far-reaching powers.

Mothers begin to adopt new methods of behavior with their children. "If you do not do as you are told, my darling, they will come and get you—and you will never see Mama and Papa again."

This seemingly toothless threat implants unintended horror in the hearts of many mischievous children and would sometimes manifest in night terrors and bed-wetting. This implicit tactic was in some ways practiced in other relationships throughout Folium, from factory owners to their laborers, the clergy to parishioners, and so on, further inflating the invisible control of the state and personifying it to a bogeyman that maintains a watchful eye on every citizen of Folium.

Each district under a soft siege receives a mighty blow, weakening morale to an unprecedented low. Even the resources that flow through Folium's economic veins suffer stagnation, but no one dares to speak up. Folium is dying a slow, anemic death, silently, yet sadistically with no collective outcry. The nurtured atmosphere of fear used to be a quivering idea, scurrying about in their homes, and could easily be stomped out by the elders' voices of reason, but the menacing beast is forcefully disarming them of their courage and will.

With no justification, communities are devastated. Members continue to disappear, feeding the growing state of terror. Even schoolchildren are victims of the paranoia that plagues the ministries. They are taken out of their classrooms in the middle of the day into vehicles of the ministry of justice and never return.

In the midst of the afternoon, in a quiet district known for its neutrality, a small boy in his school uniform—brown shorts and a lion lamb emblem on his chest—is dragged before his classmates and asked, "Are you a Magma!"

He feverishly responds, "I don't know what a Maga-gaga-mmma is, Madam."

They whip him, and he wets his pants in the presence of his classmates. The class is filled with girls wearing perfectly groomed pigtails and boys in straight razor shaves. "Peitsche, Peitsche, Peitsche!"

The director looks to the students and asks, "My children, what must we preserve?"

They shout, "Folium, Folium, Folium!"

The director raises her hand and suspends it for minutes. "What about your father or anyone else in your home?" She drills the boy with more and more questions and whips him between each reply. His playmates say, "Peitsche, Peitsche, Peitsche!

The final whips break the boy to falsely confess and agree to spy on his father. He is rewarded with a nickeled metal whistle.

For many years, this campaign of intimidation and terror remains uninterrupted in the name of peace and justice—from the classroom to the streets of every town.

Anesthetized by this recurring state of siege and terror, the people begin to adjust to this new normal. They see no way out of a condition they once agreed to at a time when patriotism was at its zenith and accept it as a justified actuality. They agreed to it as long as it was someone else and not them—those accused enemies of Folium. The patriotic response demonstrated their allegiance and love for their ministries, which seemed like a justified reaction at the time. They believed the lie as many before under similar circumstances. The state of things lasted through the next generation. The children knew nothing else but the realism they are taught, the fears they are indoctrinated with, and the lies they are innocently fed. This fundamental idea was worth forsaking personal liberties until someone else became their mothers, innocent children snatched from their mothers' bosoms, and husbands who did not return home from the mining fields. Despite the unbearable conditions of day-to-day living and their squelching hope, no one dared speak up or publicly object—lest they too disappear.

Fear enters the worship halls as well. It finds a comfortable seat among the pews and the pulpit and goes home with each parishioner at the end of every service. The elders of the districts, formerly inspired by the movements of old, are quieted and muzzled only to speak of happy speech. Members of the ministries in attendance see to it that talk of revolution is suppressed and limited to meaningless things. Hobbyists of the faith are ready to report any deviation from the state-sanctioned program and fill the pews, blending in with everyone else.

Four well-dressed men negotiate arms deals in the back pews, and the elder begins his speech with a salute to Folium—and not even one eyebrow rose.

The clergyman says, "Today, I want to speak to you about two ways to rise to greatness and find happiness as loyal servants who are willing to serve Folium's true ideals. I want to bring you to a place in your life where the pursuit of happiness becomes a reality here in Folium where the king is God and God is king. Do I hear a salute?"

The parishioners salute. "Hail the royal house, hail to her ministries, and hail to the perfect Republic of Folium!" The usual serving of loyalty to the ministers is well crafted and delivered in a spoonful of happy speech. Acquiescence is echoed in every temple. The sacred text has already been republished with critical pieces omitted or changed, leaving many none the wiser. Folium continues to receive a soft but significant strike on all fronts, and she is well on her way to becoming the vision of her rulers in plain sight—and hidden from her people. The empire is disguised as a republic and fools the people into the belief that she is a democracy where the people control the governance with fear and intimidation.

This fear does not infect everyone. It is ineffective with the young generation. A small group sees little value in remaining silent. They live by the motto "Liberty or death," and they are willing to defend it to that end.

While Folium maintains order with an iron fist and ramps up its propaganda to suppress alternative views, her eyes and ears rely heavily on ordinary citizens to serve as spies and information givers.

Operators of the Royal Junior Corps, who reformed the youth, do away with the uniforms and the infamous name and restructure her tentacles through loyal volunteers. The corps is retrained as operatives who spy on groups accused of inciting revolution. Whenever the people organize peaceful protests, the RJC manipulates the environment, cooperating with illegitimate protesters from outside districts paid to incite violence to delegitimize the cause.

In the dusty afternoons, tucked away from the city glare, nearly forgotten towns carry on with small protests—not as simulative as the rest of Folium, but evidential of the sentiments of the town. They are not as aggressive, but they are equally passionate because their condition has been worsened by cyclical poverty and broken families that move into their towns like widow spiders appearing from early spring to summer. In their minds, they are protesting figurative bondage, taking the fight to those who bind their souls.

At the end of the main highway, buses expel long lines of men from the coalmines. Toiling under the harsh conditions of the dark caves, in a gloom of despair, their broken bodies revert to the makeshift shanties for a few hours of rest. Too weak to join the protest, they silently applaud from their hearts. Before every door and open windows, they shout, "For the people, for the nation!"

The protest draws crowds from every town it enters. Each town entrance has an erected billboard that reads, "Long live the state and peace to all."

A boy coming into Boucherville with his sister says, "They might as well have written, "Long live terror!" As they return home from their underprivileged school, they stop to witness the protesters parading by with signs and chants. They return to their empty homes like many of their comrades. Their mother, like many in the village, is forced to abandon their caregiving to join the fathers in the mining fields.

The parents work from dawn until sundown, leaving their children alone and surrounded by trivial things. In Boucherville, as a once large colonial base of raw material and earth materials for Folium, destitution takes on a firm grip, squeezing the life out of the land. It remains powerless economically and politically. The only memory of her usefulness are the town entrances that carry the names of their former masters and billboards that read: "The usual mind games."

CHAPTER
SIX

• • •

Protest and Second Exodus

Y ears following the harvest and the purge of undesirables, the sentient people of Folium, mired in fanaticism, fall deeper into a state of amnesia, forgetting the actions and the state of mind that created the condition they are in. Breaking every sacred covenant guarded by their ancestors, they adopt blasphemous ideologies and lifestyles that were abandoned by those wounded of its consequence in the past. Their short-term memory continues to work against them in the restructuring and reengineering of the fundamentals of their society, the sanctum of spirituality, the divine orientation of the family, and the permissible powers of the state. Folium's disjointed unions broke apart like fragments of the firmaments, falling quickly as a fiery rock crashing into the oceans of an already dismal nation.

Quelled by a long-lasting tenet that identifies objectors and heralds as relics from the past, they create more suppressive laws to subdue the voice of those seen as alarmists to a day of judgment that will never come and mythmakers who seek to control the masses with allegorical depictions of a long-forgotten myth. Marginalized as quacks and doom-laden voices of dissension, their so-called irrelevant ideas of the past are seen as archaic and not in keeping with the progressive direction of the state. They are, therefore, methodically reassigned to districts with other groups deemed as inept, maladroit, and useless.

Years after the reconstruction, Folium is rising from a scorched earth into a high-flying creation of ingenious minds and masters of all things remarkable. The state, in its development, has successfully crushed long-lasting positions of revolt against the ministries and recycled the sentiments of betrayal of innocence to an increased love of the concept that the state is equivalent to God. Like the generation before, they fall into a spellbound grip of materialism, selfishness, and loyalty only to the state. Dancing again with the enemy of their fathers, they become like the mythical Narcissus, who fell in love with his own image and with his reflection as seen outside Folium's districts. This romancing and courting with darkness are to the tune played by the clever schemes imposed on the populace retooled for the new generation but on track for the Great Agenda. Distracted by meaningless things, they reinvent themselves. They accept repugnant ideas banished by their forefathers, and with open arms, are fated to relive the consequences. Over and over again, they worship falsehoods at the altars of ideologies that enslaved them many times before and kept them blinded to the realities that confront them.

As social scholars begin to introduce new philosophies and intellectuals pursue more knowledge, Folium opens its borders to trade of goods and foreign ideas. Ideas that would have been seen as damaging to the fabric of the republic and her sacred beliefs generations before are now integrating into her culture, language, and government.

The essence and goodness that remains in Folium are weakening from centuries of repeated mistakes and do not seem to be changing. Even the annual pilgrimage to the remote mountains by a minority of righteous people, who some believe are responsible for staving off immediate judgment, have declined in numbers. The event is replaced by activities catered to the insatiable appetite of the youth. They chant slogans that defile the name of the Most High and contort their bodies to imitate fallen creators from the outer worlds.

A handful of spiritual leaders of Folium is not deterred, however, and continues the pilgrimage with the small numbers of followers, interceding for the lost souls they see as drowning in Folium's lustful wine. These elders have not forgotten the past and remain conscious regardless of the malevolent development of the ministries and the hidden hands of the ruling elite. Among the elders are members of the Magma, who secretly work to battle the system and open the minds of the next generation.

Rising Son

When the sun's first visible rays begin to draw a golden line on the blurred horizon, a young ram emerges from the thicket of a growing bush. Wrestling with the spiny gray thorns and bleating along with the sheep behind him, framed in by a rickety wooden fence, it successfully emerges from its bondage. Above them, the sky yields to the early morning the new day as two red birds begin to chirp. On the rooftops and between the dusty alleys, all seems tranquil. A kite tangled in a tree occasionally rattles as a small wind blows.

A man opens his shutters slightly, squinting away from the linear rays of the sun as it pierces through the miniscule opening. He tries to draw a mental picture from the small frame and subtle morning sounds, but there is not enough information to determine what's happening outside.

In curiosity, he opens the neglected shutters for a better look, but he still cannot see much. Its squeaky hinge worries him as he indecisively ponders if he should close them or leave them as they are.

"What are you looking for out there?" asks his wife. She begins to open her eyes to the direct rays of the sun.

"I can't tell for sure, my dear, but I believe another house has been marked."

"For enlisting with the local church?" she asks.

"I am not sure, darling, but I feel uneasy at the moment. It's like someone is wandering outside, but I can't tell much without attracting attention to the house."

His wife says, "Maybe it's the rats rummaging through the trash again."

He quickly replies, "Perhaps, but it just doesn't feel right." He closes the old shutters and returns to his bed. His eyes remain fixated on the imaginary patterns in the ceiling. At that moment, a fig nut from an overreaching fruit tree lands on their rooftop, bounces twice, and rolls down to their front porch.

"What was that?" He grips the edge of their bed.

"What? What? What?" She sits up and looks through the window. "What did you hear, my husband?"

Soon, the silence of dusk falls back to the sounds of a crowing rooster and then another falling fig. The man jumps from his disheveled bed and stands. "The writing is on the wall, my dear! The hour is changing, and I can't remain asleep any longer." With hands gesturing the absoluteness of his decision, he runs to another window closer to the rear of the house, frantically looking for evidence of movement outside. Still unable to gain a sense of the happenings outside, he runs to the kitchen and uncovers the unleavened bread in search for something he must have hidden there. He searches other irrational places and tiptoes to a small ladder to reach the upper cabinets for a hidden device that he must have saved there for an event such as this. He finds a small golden dinner bell from the last harvest. He climbs down with the bell and places it near the unleavened bread. Disappointed and biting his lips from the growing angst, he paces back and forth until he stubs his toe on the edge of a tall wooden cabinet. Upon leaning on the doors for support, it opens wide—and out fall two of the tools of his labor. He reaches past a sickle and grabs a weighty black hammer. With a hammer in one hand and a sickle in other, he anxiously waits for what is to come next. He waits for hours until the red sun begins to rise, and his shadow begins to cast an unusual image on the kitchen table.

His wife soon reluctantly enters the kitchen and immediately sees the striking silhouette of a man wearing a crown and holding a hammer and a distorted spike. Then she quickly looks up where he stands and sees him motionlessly standing in the path of dusty rays of the sun. Like stunned prey, his countenance remains unchanged—and his eyes remain fixed outside their window. He doesn't utter a word as his fists tightly grip his overused farming tools. His glazed eyes fixate past the window and give in to the visions in his mind's eye, which reveals a paradigm shift of a hunter stealthily attacked by camouflaged prey.

Full of emotion, his wife calls out his name, "Asa! Asa!"

He doesn't respond verbally. He slightly tilts his head to hear what she has to say. Abruptly, a campaign of ministry trucks races by, lifting more dust in the air and creating a gray cloud of obscurity and dimness. He whispers, "The raiders are here. The raiders are here. The raiders are here."

Later in the afternoon, radios around Boucherville, the squares of Bidonville, and in the countryside systematically begin to announce breaking news of a fire at the ministry of justice. They purport that the arson attack was planned and executed by the elders of the religious district and a sect minority previously disposed of outside the major districts. A robotic voice dispenses a list of violations previously documented by the ministries as punishable by termination and declares that they will capture the conspirators this time.

The revered prime officiate promises to bring Folium's enemies to justice and changes the tone of the broadcast to one of solidarity. "People of Folium, the beloved patriots of the state and the motherland, lend me your ears and hear me say that today what we have witnessed is a beacon from heaven that shines as bright as the stars of Continuum. I have prophesied this to you before, and many did not believe." He shouts as though weeping for a lost loved one, "I have cried out from the squares, but you did not harken to my warnings, but today ... today, you have seen with your own eyes. Today is the day we all must unite to fight a common enemy." He breaks the melancholy tone with a sudden rage as one who has found the assailant who has harmed his proverbial beloved.

"My brothers and sisters, lend me your hearts, your love, your loyalty, and I will bring you into a new age where peace and harmony live in absoluteness. Lend me your will, and I will show you what I see—a world where there are no factions and division of districts, where our enemies will have no power to harm us again. Are you with me, my beloved?"

Around many radios, members of Folium shout at the unresponsive speakers. "Yes! Yes! Yes!" They salute with their right arms in the air. "Long live Folium!"

"I have declared a state of emergency and a cessation of the charters to address the emerging crisis. This decree will in no form endanger our protected liberties, but it will provide the basis by which our agents may pursue the enemies within our borders and outside our borders, the enemies who have declared war on Folium. Let this decree serve as an advertisement to those who would harbor, protect, or conceal the enemies of the state. A friend of our enemy is an enemy of Folium. My people, what say you?"

The nationalist chorale begins to play in the background.

"Long live Folium! Long live Folium! Long live Folium!"

Within hours of the broadcast, the ministry institutes a mass arrest on all declared as enemies of the state. In a little town in Roulerville, a Hebrew man and his family are dragged out from under their bed and into the glass-littered streets.

An angry mod circles them with clubs and broken glass bottles. "Long live Folium!"

His brother lives across town and frantically runs out from his vehicle as rocks fly into his windows. He is struck by a wooden cross and is motionless beneath the cross.

Miles away, in the hills, a group of children is pushed to the ground as they exit the Iconia. "Yeshua! Yeshua! Yeshua!"

"Long live Folium!"

In Bidonville, a rock is hurled into a cathedral, narrowly missing a priest as he concludes evening Mass. All throughout Folium, the hunt commences to find and attack people suspected as followers of the holy faith, followers of the Most High.

Elders Meet

The following month, an emergency meeting is called by the top elders of the Bidonville District to prepare a written response to the ministry of justice and a call to the clergymen for an exodus if need be. Small factions begin to form organized protests in front of government buildings, but this becomes an absolute failure and only prolongs the assault on the believers and a strangling compromise between the temple and the state.

Among the educated youth, a spirit of revolt ignites like a spark. It rises from the sleepy towns like a mountain from a turbulent sea to confront the collective sentiment of the aggressors. By the mere mention of the random acts of violence on the radio, university students organize groups and march to the squares in protest. Several groups representing the same persecution meet at the square.

"We will not go quietly into the night when they say, 'Go home!' No! We will not retreat to the comforts of our homes when they say, 'Go home.' No! We will not retreat while we, as well as our brothers and sisters, are stricken day and night because of imposed classifications, such as our race, faith, or political faction."

A student stands on a large rock. "What say you, my fellow citizen?" They cry out, "Revolution! Revolution! Revolution!"

A sea of young men and women rush the pillars of the square and rattle the grounds until the early morning.

This new revolution incited by a new generation of Folium comes at a moment when the emotional fatigue of the old renders them inept to action. They are not as thoroughly well read in the writings of sojourners of the *Mosaic* or informed of the hidden hand that works against them, but they are equipped with a longing for justice. Their fathers and mothers, thoroughly indoctrinated, can no longer see or hear the war cries of the young arguing their position and warning them of the risk of opposing the ministries. The youth sedition trickles down the remote mountains unto the four districts of Folium, Roulerville, Slogtown, Bidonville, and Boucherville.

Older men sent down by the Magma lead the students, direct small pockets of protesters to various civic locations in each district, and create a string of strategic demonstrations. Some of the women had been asked to manufacture black and brown bags that conceal the sacred texts used in the gatherings and frequently read by the seniors to the groups before each outpost as they head out.

There are many husbands and sons who secretly meet in the forests and barns to discuss orders sent to them by the elders. They hand out flyers written by loyal brothers of the faith, who through association of the Order of Magma, serve them news and strategies. At its pinnacle, their policies lead to a contagious unrest. Protest hits the busy streets of the squares as fear is replaced with frustration, righteous anger, and awareness.

In Bidonville, men, women, and youths gather with fiery rage in their eyes. They shout, "Long live freedom! Long live freedom! Long live our freedom!" They meet at crossroads where opposing points of view direct them to return home, but they are not deterred by the intimidation. As the sum of their collective experiences and armed by patriotic zeal, like that one recorded in the books written by their forbearers, they march on. They shout, "For the people! For the nation!"

Both the unconscious and semiconscious, the restless masses, maneuver around a center fountain situated below a large iconic statue. It personifies the endless essence of Folium and its struggles in that they are like Sisyphus as he trundles a boulder uphill only to have it roll back upon them, repeatedly and endlessly. A maddening cycle. There, the heavy cast-iron statue reminds discernible countrymen of their upward struggle. The boulder is a wheel that spins upward on a mountain or hill that is too steep for conquest. Surrounding the monument and on rooftops, more agitated people stand by, growing in numbers and making their presence known with chants. Confusion is swarming in the square—some for and others against the decision to terminate presumed spies, persecution of the followers of the Most High, and other changes in Folium.

"By their roots, we will know them!" shouts one stout man. Another voice from the rear echoes the same, inciting the excited mass. More shouts rumble from the nest. Emotion thickens the air as their determination increases with every hour. Semiconscious overtakes the cause and they cry for justice. Their roar increases, crashing into the seams of the city walls.

More shouts fill the air. "We are a people, one people not divided! We stand here to uproot and cast and burn the ones who corrupt and destroy us!" Tight fist jabs forward as though fighting an invisible foe. "By their roots, we will know them! We stand united. By their roots, we will know them! We stand united!" Jab after empty jab into the air, they endure. The roots the conscious speak of are not that of the foretold heroes of Folium—but the generation of scandalous men of Folium. The semiconscious see their countrymen as potential enemies and begin to argue and shout toward the conscious. A clergyman climbs a rock and starts to bawl through a ram's horn. "My people ... my people ... do not do this! We cannot stand united if we fight amongst ourselves. My people!"

Few people stop to listen to the clergyman's plea.

Large stretching branches providing shade to spectators from across the square, bounce and rattle as people fill the streets, forcing others to higher ground. Erupting with slogans and songs and waving banners, students stretch over the enmeshed people below. The uprising is reaching its capacity and heating up rapidly. The exuberance could shift the mass into a violent crusade at any moment. A selfless grievance at the onset served as a catalyst for a change but has since been used as a platform for all sorts of societal ailments. They are a people visibly divided.

What brings them to the busy streets under the imperfect weather is the contention that the newly ratified law had unraveled into a new form of serfdom and was denigrating the people into further regression between sects and ethnic groups. The displaced found themselves in districts based on matrices gathered from the census they completed a decade before. Siblings from the same home were living regions apart, separated by data and criteria farmed by the ministry of truth.

No longer a docile and passive people, they are besieged by tenuous governance and grow weary of the conditions of the day. Perpetual scarcity is plentiful, and the loss of hope is unavoidable. Folium's slippery slide away from the moral standards it once held in high regard and the takeover from degenerate ideology created a dismal outlook. It has become a repugnant state, and it is burdened with an enormous national debt that cracks the backs of those under generational poverty. Disparity in the middle class and poor is becoming indistinguishable. A class is just a euphemism—not an actual designation of achievement or lack thereof. Food subsidies in communities with plenty of cropland to feed its people by many folds were redistricted for capital redistribution to outside republics. Folium has become an incorporated state, private property to conglomerates, diminished into stock rather than a collective community. It could barely hold the basis that solidified the people. Profit is crowned as supreme king while integrity futilely begs at the steps of the royal courts.

Rising like a tide pouring out from sleepy and unsuspecting corners of the cities, the conscious plead their case to the presiding ministries, ministry of justice, agriculture, and truth for amelioration, a change to their circumstances. "By their roots, we will know them! By their roots, we will know them!" The shouts continue, and so does the opposition. Their roar is deafening and can be heard for several miles outside the square.

Anxiously moving about the innumerous people, a protective young apprentice from the local university shelters a barely visible young woman, shielding her body with his. The turmoil did not abate their participation, but they are cautious nonetheless. They wear their school's crest and colors, khaki bottoms and white tops displaying a fighting lion. Neatly folded under their arms are unused banners for the protest. They remain hidden as they evade potential conflict. Small pockets in the group that want to start trouble begin to hurl objects recklessly at the protesters and stores. This further invalidates the protest to onlookers, turning it into another perceived riot of ruffians and outside hooligans.

Alerted of the unrest when word makes it to the desk of the ministries, General Enthous—previously deposed of his duties under the ministry of truth—is tasked with suppressing the protest and sustaining justice. He orders an infantry to secure critical points of the square. Racing against time, the couple maneuvers around the gridlock and incoming rocks that cut through shuttered windows and abandoned vehicles. Desperately needing to regain their wits and breath, they run to a safe area under a green canopy. They hope not to be discovered by the vagrants. The worst of the events is over—or at least the opposition or government authorities aren't pursuing them, but they need to leave the area quickly.

Reimonde whispers, "I saw this before, or maybe it was déjà vu. No, it was in a dream, a changing timeline. It was right here. No, over there by the banyan tree. Many of them dangled like rags. Hurry. We have to leave this place. Now! The situation is only going to get worse. It's unpredictable at this point."

The protest, from his point of view, is amounting to wayfaring. People have slogans and banners, and onlookers foolishly wait like sitting ducks. It has become a menagerie of unhinged emotions that only means trouble.

Further fueling fear and confusion, the hooligans decide it is a good idea to shoot into the air.

"For what benefit? Perhaps only to appease their emotions—but nothing else. The protest is a lost cause. It is all for naught," Reimonde says.

Hidden among the colossal band of angry men, women, and organized groups peddling political antics, they spot their vehicle. They dash to the unmarked silver vehicle near a drainage slope. Their classmates shout from the automobile, "Reimonde! Madine! Hurry!" They enter quickly and disappear behind the jagged rubble and towering buildings.

Behind them, faint roars and warlike cries fade in the presence of the countryside road. "Folium! Folium! Folium!"

At the square, the air—heated and thickened with aggressive emotions—shrouds the unsuspecting semiconscious and conscious from noticing the band of armed forces closing off the roads. In a split second, the counter force seizes the perimeters, making its way into the square.

General Enthous, wiping his nose with a red handkerchief, spits on the ground and orders an attack. "There will be no more of this trouble. This ends today!" He shouts to his men for an increase to the onslaught. Dissatisfied with the results, he yanks one of the ray guns from a member of his infantry and focuses it directly at a little girl neatly dressed in red. Holding a queen rag doll and desperately tugging on her mother's hem as they both run through the crowd, she calls out to her mother. Both are hit with the first wave and fall to the ground. The girl begins to scream as her mother remains motionless on the ground. She falls beside her mom and whimpers.

"More, more, more!" The general points to others climbing through broken windows.

In that moment, ringing breaks through the protestors, piercing above the ruckus of the mass like a vibrant thunderbolt and wading through an agitated sea of people. In panic and confusion, the gathering disseminates in various directions, frantically searching for a crack to squeeze through. In agony to the painful and nauseating sonic beam, they screech and yell, tightly sealing their burning ears. Some fall to the ground from the thermos effects and others as a result of the inundating waves. Grasping each other like suffocating fish absent of water, many hundreds crawl to unclogged passages. Scattered about and ripping through bushels with every shred of hope left to return to their homes alive, they flee like animals from a slaughterhouse. They run through alleys, and some try to escape into wall openings.

The others with the presence of mind and physical ability, they head for the mountains. Like those before them who had fled decades ago during the great migration, they leave their trappings behind. They understand the grim reality staring them in the face. These are the few who rejected ideologies that purported a false sense of security and sustainability in Folium. Recognizing that they were not entirely free, they search for and gain a new consciousness. They understand that they are merely slaves to a system that will exterminate them once their usefulness ends.

It is a wise choice on their part. They would have easily been identified in the demonstration by their embroidered crests and permits issued by the state for a lawful congregation. Behind them, in the square, a hazy film of ash impermeable by the bright, scorching sun bathes the dazed protesters. The government authorities release smoke canisters and more microwaves to detain the rioters who could not run away.

Folium would never be the same. Turning their faces forward, the escapees look toward freedom and the shelter of the concealed mountains.

The Camps

Later in the afternoon, truckloads of dissidents arrive at the ministry's courtyard to face the magistrate in session. Well-organized lines in front of under-ventilated pods greet them. The day's mood is melancholy and gray. In front of each pod, representatives of the magistrate process the new prisoners.

"Number 93! Please present yourself before the court." From behind the second stage line, an endless stream of lines awaits trial.

A prisoner is lured into the magistrate's chamber with his hands firmly tied and a tight muzzle on his face.

"You are at this moment sentenced to District AC603 to serve the terms outlined in your implant. You must maintain these implants at all times and be ready to present them when commanded. How do you wish to wear your upload? I can either have it imprinted on your arm or port it to your chip."

Number 93 unfolds his cold, pale hands and stretches them slightly outward to receive the implant.

An agent beside the magistrate begins rapidly typing on his holographic computer. "He has been integrated, Your Honor."

The magistrate says, "The information contained in this program and any accompanying codes may contain privileged, private, and confidential information protected by the state of Folium. Any attempt to dismember, alter, or remove your implant will result in the break of primary and secondary links to the central signatures on the system, thereby negating the privileges and freedoms afforded to you by the state—not limited to termination of life. Do you understand?"

Prisoner 93 nods in agreement and is ushered away from of the bench. The next prisoner is summoned as number 93 joins his compatriots.

"Next prisoner, step forward!"

The stomping of several feet is followed by a desperate plea.

"Your magistrate, please, I am an innocent bystander, having nothing to do with the protestors … have mercy on your servant!"

The magistrate responds, "So, I have before me a coward and a liar. Folium has no use for the kind." She snaps her fingers, and the prisoner hits the ground "Next prisoner, step forward!"

At the processing station, a prominent pod is guarded by agents of the magistrate. Inside, pod U113, an accused leader of the opposition is called to stand before an assigned advocate. He is visibly weak and malnourished. He has not groomed his beard or changed his clothes for quite some time.

"Good morning, Number 78. I am Ms. AI. I am here to represent you with your case and see to your transition toward your appointed district with expediency and efficiency. How are you this glorious day, sir?" Without looking up to see his irritated face or pausing long enough for an answer, she dives straight into her metal briefcase. "I trust I have found you well despite your condition? Wonderful. Let us begin with some primary business." With a nervous snicker, she says, "I am returning from thirty-six other cases that did not turn out quite the way I planned. The stubborn nature of people makes my work difficult, but a stubborn allegiance to greed makes it that much more difficult. Please pardon my lack of preparation as I search for your file. You were just assigned to me this morning. I trust our meeting will be eventful and you will find solace in the outcome. Yes?"

Joshua does not answer.

She skims over her other cases in search of Joshua's case. "Let me look through these folders. Give me a moment." She browses through tabs of folders and files in search of his assigned number and then pauses to read a document. "There! Mr. Joshua, Prisoner 78. I have these forms that require your bio-signature, and then we can begin."

"What is the nature of your visit here, Ms. AI?"

Ms. AI nervously smiles, adjusts her skirt, and takes a seat across from Joshua's weary body. Casually folding her legs, she leans back in a galvanized military chair and studies the layout of the metallic pod and the ceiling's rib-like joints. Gazing at the hardened dirt floor, she moves her eyes up to the prisoner's tattered shoes, which are strung together by stretching shackles. "Good evening, Number 78. I was assigned your case to assist you with matters concerning your containment. I aim to do just that, but you must first sign these documents if I am to help you." Leaning forward, she hurriedly says, "There are procedures for this process, and if I am to work with them, you must first be willing to work with me. How do you choose to proceed, Number 78?"

Joshua firmly replies, "I choose liberty!"

After a short pause, he lifts his head and stares into her eyes. "I will not be complicit in the plans of your kings if that is your mission. I have already stated my plea. Regardless if the pawns they send come to me with a smile, I stand firm in my conviction."

Ms. AI says, "Number 78! Whether you live or die, Folium will remain Folium. She is more than one man, one flag, or one creed. You decide today how you choose to live or die. I am only a conduit to your liberation and cannot promise you one iota of hope unless you agree to endorse these documents. As an active advocate of the prisoners in this camp, I can only advise you of your outcome based on your acquiescence or lack thereof. I sincerely hope you are aware that your allegiance to a dying creed can cost you more than just your liberty."

Grinding his teeth, Joshua responds, "I would have you know, Ms. AI, that my creed teaches me a time-relevant truth that I cannot expect you to understand. You have been defiled by the lies of this system and could not see it even if you tried. I only ask that you submit my plea before the magistrate for the right to resume as a regular citizen of Folium—free to practice my faith without any impediments."

He takes a deep breath, tilts his head, and looks toward the entrance. "I refuse to live like this ... as a fugitive in my own land, padded away like a dangerous animal in this forsaken cave. They carried me away from my home to this place to break me. This cage is where I eat, sleep, and defecate. I spend hours on my back at night, staring into nothingness and creating some resemblance of hope in my mind, but it remains very dim. Let me tell you something, miss, before they began their investigation into my affiliation with the religious factions and ties to the Magma or the districts I visited, they marked me as a wanted man, well before, simply because of my faith. I appealed to the ministries with my certified papers, but they didn't want to hear from me because, all along, it had nothing to do with the legalities they purport to defend. They had already made up their minds that I was an enemy of the state. I am a nonentity to them ... just a member of an undesired mass. Five days, I stood in those long lines waiting to be seen—only to be denied again and again. Five long days without proper food or housing. I traveled as a nomad, going from place to place, here and there to a trail of tears, as it were. I was like a bound man retracing his tracks in a triangular route to meet their demand in this so-called process. Nearly broken by the sheer anguish, I came to the realization I am, but a man on a fruitless quest. .

"Endorsing your document today would be a dishonor of everything I stood for—an insult to my family, my ancestors. I have done what they have asked and now demand that they do as I have asked. I have been inundated with their transgenic programming before and recognize it well, madam. They know very well what they are doing by sending you here. It is no coincidence that your name resembles the artificial intelligence that integrated souls into the system in the early century."

Joshua's voice begins to quiver as he relives the situation in his mind. "They are trying to destroy my will to fight! This crafty scheme they so perfectly use against me and everyone else against the system has nullified me into what you see today, a tattered frame, but I stand firm in my conviction nonetheless. The imprudent kings of Folium have sacked this land and many like it where the lustful power of their greed drives every agenda, every declaration of war, and every decree. Never have they upheld the honor of the sacred codes. The people of Folium, like loyal sheep, follow them into war, blindly offering their lives as collateral to pay the debt it creates. In the end, they learn that the ubiquitous doctrine of war is the same. In my life, I have only seen the unrighteousness of war, which always comes to one end, to fill the purse of the crown and her servants. Never does it serve the honorable, the noble, and the innocent. I have yet to see a war that preserves the liberty of its people—only wars that kill for profit in the name of the citizens. Wars safeguard the riches of the land and kill the people who inhabit it. Ms. AI, as I stated before, I choose liberty— liberty for every tribe, every clan, every family, and for every man."

Ms. AI replies, "Rubbish! You have been misguided in this notion, drawing conclusions that have no merit. You would be a fool not to compromise with the state. Your date has already been set, and it is going to be too late for you. You are not a fugitive, and Folium has not declared war against you. It is you who have declared war on Folium. You are, in effect ... how should I put this? You are a man living on a hiatus of reality perpetuated by myths and false hopes. Men like you see women like me as the forgotten Lilith and contrive stories to cover it up in your book. Your people are full of conspiracies and lies. When you finally decide to accept what is real and the demands of the ministries, you will be a free man once again."

"Lies, you say? Hmmm … if you want to help me, you can start by having them suspend my case based on my original appeal. I refuse to continue like this. I am not an animal. I am a free man, even now, at least in my mind. Those malevolent ones are trying to steal my essence by connivance, by convincing me to oblige to more and more of their schemes. They are lies! I won't, I tell you. I will not do it."

"What do you mean?" Ms. AI asks. "I am not sure I understand what you are saying here. I do not comprehend what you are saying to me. What do you mean by *essence*?"

With both hands on his head, he replies, "I am telling you that I am a member of Magma, a follower of the Christ. I have a unique code in me. They want to activate the Folium chip, and they need my bio-signature to achieve it. Unless I agree, they are going to keep me here indefinitely. They sent you here to coerce me into accepting their terms on the basis of a compromise. My rights to practice outside the exiled districts has very little to do with it. It's about control. I just won't accept those terms."

"And what are these terms, Number 78? I am sure they are no different from everyone else's loyalty to the state?"

Rubbing his face, Joshua responds, "I am carrying the weight of a thousand kings, and you come before me with delusionary solutions and ask me questions with the weight of a feather. You have not the slightest idea, do you, miss? It's the helix. It's the map they are after. They have always been in the pursuit of the map—the cryptic code inside my makeup. The same one is written in the universe, divinely written to protect the Most High's perfect plan." He mutters, "It is forbidden to cross this sacred seal of life with a third." Looking at the double-ribbed joints in the pods and the shadows moving about outside, he says, "Good day, madam!" He turns his back to the appointed advocate.

Ms. AI says "Number 78! Thank you for your cooperation. We have worked finely today, and I trust you will be transitioned to your appointed district with expediency and efficiency. Good day, sir." Brushing her hair from her right helix to behind her earlobe, she ducks her head and walks outside. While glancing back at the frail man who seems determined not to proceed with orders delivered from the ministries, she mutters, "Cross with a third? What does that have to do with anything?" She walks past the guards and heads toward the next pod: Atomic Unit U115.

CHAPTER
SEVEN

⋆⋆⋆

Exodus: The Climb

L ooking back to assess the distance gained during her climb, a pretentious middle-aged woman swaddled in fine linen and a blue head scarf trots across the deserted country roads in search of a refuge. The brilliance of the sun shining on the crown of her head pales her surroundings to a hue of gray. She is uncomplicated in her appearance, but she is aptly dressed given her unplanned departure. Moving with elegance and grace, she maintains her posture despite the midday's sandy wind.

With the few personal effects she could carry in her escape from the quaint villas of Roulerville, she secures the burdensome sack across her shoulder, shifting the weight of the book it holds from one shoulder to the other. After miles of walking under the unforgiving sun, she rests her travel staff on the rich black soil and pauses to catch her breath.

Holding onto her narrow waist and sturdy staff for stability, she lets out a long and profound exhale. Raising her bent shoulders and stretching her ornamented neck as though pulling out optimism from her tired and dehydrated body, she lets out another deep sigh. As though having birth pains, she wets her lips, bites on her bottom lip, and squeezes the staff. Breathing heavily from her mouth and exhaling through her nose, she lowers her head as the sweat from her brow drips to the ground.

Long nights under cascading willow trees and treading through shallow creeks drains her of the will to continue, but her resolve is that of many fleeing from the squares. She leaves all material things behind and preserves her life. Omi is one of the many who was forcefully subjective to the law recently passed in Bidonville. One of Folium's largest agriculture districts, it provides foodstuffs to locals and foreign district conglomerates. Toiling on the private farms of Bidonville with sack aproned around their waists and necks, the divested peasants dot the landscape, following a steady quota demanded by the landowners. They worked on hectares of flat land sprouted with rich legumes, adjoining rolling green hills of cocoa and coffee beans. Daily, large unmarked trucks entered the district via unpaved back roads to the widening corridors of the packing plants. The largest, owned by a prominent family with ties to the ministries, has inscribed *NOS* on the entry post. Tugging at its base were two statues— one of a lion and the other a sort of wild mutated beast. It resembles the logo printed on leaflets suspiciously found at the square.

Just as quickly as they arrived, the ironclad trucks race out with large barrels of cocoa, coffee beans, grains, and tealeaves, bundled and labeled with names of landlords across Folium. The diesel trucks rock on the bumpy roads, funneling past the shantytowns where the malnourished workers live and back to the bustling port.

Bidonville delicately balances production and consumption. Bidonville's stakeholders uprooted her essence and repurposed her land to a conveyor belt, exporting hard-earned capital to outside interests.

Omi recalls those hard times experienced by the workers in the fields and how the circumstance was not an isolated event. It eventually crept up to the middle class to a segment of the population that failed to heed the warning signs. As a respected matriarch of the community and owner of a recently seized banana plantation, Omi's reluctance to flee was reversed rather quickly and surprisingly on a dreadful night—on the eve of the great harvest. She was awakened by arguments outside her gated villa and came face to face with a reality she never thought she would encounter. While quite infrequently, disturbances in her area were never more than petty disagreements between neighbors or families celebrating a graduation a bit too late in the evening for her taste, but none required intervention. She would often ignore them in the comfort of her home with the assurance it would end soon, but this time, it could not be overlooked.

In a close inspection, peering through the cracks of her drapes, she could see a white-knuckled man held by his collar, completely filled with fear and begging for his life.

Trembling in her dimly shaded evening gown, his wife cried out to the men standing over her devastated husband. Nearly clutching their rifles, she dropped to the ground and begs for their mercy. Reaching out for their legs, she grew more frantic and crazed with the overwhelming situation and their lack of compromise. Screaming at the top of her lungs, she cried out for their humanity, but there didn't seem to be any to plead to.

Omi knew of their horrible reputation and feared for the couple's lives. When the wife's plea did not yield any favorable results, she placed herself on the truck's metal guardrails and pleaded again for mercy. She waved her arms and begged for the abuse to stop, but they kicked him and battered his head. Her screams grew louder, piercing Omi's ears with the horrific sound of fear at the draw of a broad-bladed machete. Omi turned her face. She could not bear the sight of what was about to happen. In a numbing disbelief, she thought about how the tragedy would leave the widowed woman as a broken soul in a land that seemed to be changing right before her eyes. *Maybe if I scream too, I could divert the attention away from them and to me. Perhaps that would grant them some grace to escape their captives—but that would only make me a victim. If I could aim straight for their helmets and strike their heads, but that would make them the victims.*

When she could think of nothing else, Omi began to pray. "Aba Father, great and merciful God, I plead with you at this hour that you intervene in this dreadful situation and save this man's life."

As she prayed, the machete found its target. With a sudden whack, she heard an alarming yelp that could only mean one thing: the worst possible outcome for such an undeserving family. As she wiped the tears from her dilating eyes, she took a final peek and found a bladeless machete beside a large book the man held above his head. Kneeling in a puddle of urine, he wept from the near miss.

To Omi's surprise, the man miraculously survived—only to witness his wife striving to escape from a mental loop of hysteria. In her native tongue, she cried, "They killed him. They killed him."

As an indigene of the north district who relocated near the plantations as part of their mission, she assumed a significant risk in sharing her faith so openly. She became deranged by the experience. Unlike Omi, they attracted suspicion from begrudging neighbors when their undercover work began to draw larger numbers. Their circle spoke of the Infinite, who called his people into submission and obedience of the sacred texts written in the *Book of Wisdom and Salvation*. The emergent sect was permitted to operate as long they identified themselves with the royal seal and obtained proper permits. They continued unabated until someone alerted the ministries.

The frightened woman tried to control her crying and uttered random words. As her husband held her, she regained her senses and whimpered, "Commander, he is a clergyman. Yes, my beloved is a clergyman, our visas, our papers they all say he is an elder of the religious district. Look at them. I can go inside and show you. Please, please, Commander."

The commander replied, "You knew very well what you were doing and deliberately broke the law at the brook because you believe that you are above the laws that govern this district."

"What brook, sir? The river where the merchants meet? No. No, sir. Please, sir. We respect the authority of the ministry who authorized the meeting. You will see from our papers that we are permitted, Commander. We complied with the law, sir. No … no … no! Ah!"

Falling on deaf ears, her plea moved none of his men to action. The portly commander leaned toward the wife and stared into her teary eyes, rapidly beating chest, and dangling arms. "Sarafina! Sarafina! Sarafina!"

The clergyman's wife reminded him of his younger sister who also had precarious bravado about her. Both women shared a resemblance from his vantage point. Her smooth cafe au lait skin glistened under the moonlight, partially covered by her marabou hair provided a sharper view of her visage. She had innocence in her eyes that only the moonlight was able to reveal in the dark night. Astonished by the turn of events, Omi covered her mouth in disbelief.

He whispered into her ears, "The law, Sarafina! You have not begun to understand, you poor, confused little girl. Why have you allowed yourself to become a servant among the weak, foolish, and misguided?" He wiped the profuse sweat from his face, secured his weapon on his waist, and grabbed her wrist. "Are you a lunatic? You never had a clue about the changes that were happening around you. You never could see it—even though I tried to tell you. You are still naive, Sarafina."

As though snapping out of the delusion of his sister, he elevated his voice, "We are the writers and executions of the law! We *are* the law!" He turned to one of his men in the vehicle and motioned for him to bring him something. The loyal militant, hiding behind his dark designer glasses, seemed eager to perform the deed asked of him. He removed the facade as he approached the commander.

Despite the poorly lit streets, Omi could see into his eyes and felt she was looking into the eyes of a man who have long lost his soul.

"Take him to the gallows," the commander ordered. "And you, woman, I don't know what charm saved you tonight, but I suggest that you return to your broods—or we will be forced to take the rest of you as well." The men struggled to lift the clergyman to his feet and dragged him into the vehicle. Astonishingly, they began to feel a sense of nausea weakening their will. Foaming at the mouth, they gasped and suddenly vomited every bit of what they had eaten that night.

With one hand on his holster, the commander shrugged off the woman and turned to look at his men with astonishment. Restraining the raging veins in his neck, he held his pistol in the air, lowering it to the woman's head for what seemed like an eternity. The image of his sister must have entered his mind again, as it was hard to continue with his intimidation, and relieved her of her distress. He aggressively returned his weapon to his holster, ground his teeth in disappointment, and attended to the suffering men.

The squabble was interrupted by a cracking sound across the cul-de-sac. The men quickly turned their heads in Omi's direction as the drapes quickly shuffled back to a close. Breathing as though her lungs were imploding, Omi's back remained against the bedroom wall while the cries from the frightened woman muffled behind her.

Not wanting to be targeted herself, she grabbed what she could muster, ran out the back door, and hid in her garden. She was relieved when the heavy steel doors slammed shut and the engines erupted. The trucks reversed, slowly circled the cul-de-sac, and eventually drove away. Omi remained hidden under the protection of the black night and thick vegetation.

The clergyman's wife was motionless on the gravel-filled potholes. Tears streamed down her flushed cheeks, and her husband knelt a few feet from her, dumbstruck by the terrifying interrogation. An urgent prayer and an image of seraphim spared a life that night—and perhaps even her own.

Her cries echo in Omi's mind as she continues her climb. Rumors began brewing in Roulerville after that night and eventually became a terrifying reality she continues to relive in her mind.

Interrogations, kidnappings, and roundups were sprouting through the districts and creating a frenzy in many homes. It reached a level of panic that school-aged children were instructed to walk in groups and run if approached by strangers. Some were provided silver whistles that looped around their necks, hidden behind their blue plaited lapels. As news circulated around the districts, word of the roundups slowly made it to the hills. This did not sit well with the majority. Regardless of visual observations, it was quite clear that tyranny was coming upon them. Their influence staved off some events here or there, but the larger scheme was building momentum faster than they could control.

Heated debates among commoners and intellectuals in the universities increased, but it remained no more than discussions. It was unclear if the reason for the roundups were to reorganize migrating communities, religious sects, or objectors of the new legislation. Many rumors circulated from one district to the next—with a broad spectrum of opinions. Some theories were so outrageous that they quelled action on the part of those sitting on the fence. Some ideas piqued their curiosity—but nothing more. This quickly killed any thoughts of preparedness or prudent actions that were irrespective to the gradual compromises they previously accepted. They dismissed it altogether and continued with the business of their day. Besides, the ideas were so unconventional and not in keeping with the direction Folium was heading that they were seen as lunacy. Life could not have been any better for the rising middle class. It was ludicrous to think otherwise. Although there had been small indications of something amiss, they were not significant enough to come to such conclusions. Giving time and energy to such maniacal talk of a failing Folium was a waste of time. The cathedrals were filled during the harvest, and sectarian gatherings were under control. Folium had never been greater.

At dusk, Omi makes her way to the gathering place. Fatigue is tugging at her progress and weighing down her bag. While the trail before her is shorter than what she left behind, the path is getting longer and more arduous. It is too long for an elderly and physically fatigued woman seeking sanctuary from a tiring expedition. She pauses again to take in the calmer wind.

Embracing her arm from behind, a young stoutly man carrying a rugged travel bag picks up her mangled baggage for her. He places his hand on her hunched back and encourages her to continue. With a smile, he points to the rest of the refugees ahead of them and urges her to proceed. She couldn't see what he was steering her to, but she trusted that he knew the way.

"The river is not too far from here, madam. You can drink some water and rest when we get there, but we have to hurry."

They disappear under the broad blades of tropical greengage and loosely hanging vines. Arriving at the riverbank along with the others, they navigate through the smog-covered body of water that divides the borders. Sparkling water drips from the dark green foliage and ripples on the slow river, reflecting their faces as they dip their tattered bodies into it.

Young and old hold belongings above their heads and march past a hollow tree with lush, hanging moss and colorful plants. A few continue on, and some decide to rest on the bank for the remainder of the night.

Wiping her face with a wrinkled handkerchief, Omi begins to question the young man. As she starts to describe her plight, she smiles. "Young man, thank you for your help today. You know, you remind me of my estranged son, who assuredly now sleeps on the cold floors of the camps. He has the same assuredness as you." She focuses on the young man's wooly brow. "From which region did you escape, my son? Was it the first to impose the law?" Before the young man can reply, she says, "It was rumored that our region was on the brink of raids and those found without their papers or accused of professing their faith without a permit were being huddled into trucks by men smoking calumet pipes. We called them the Calumets. Sealed shoulder patches ready to do the will of their masters— have you seen the type? Ruthless they are. Never did I think I would live to see the day of roundups and centralized farming camps." She pulls out a small black and white image of her son. "I really miss my son. Can you see the resemblance?" She shrugs and shakes her head in disillusionment. "Even worship halls are no longer safe for a weary soul. You can't tell the difference between the ruffians and the common man anymore. Everyone is afraid of his neighbors—children practically still nursing can be turned into conspirators. It is awful. It is terrible times we live in. The basis of it all was if one would dare challenge the law … you know about the law? Everyone does these days, and every one of them asked for it. They voted for it, but without really knowing what they were voting for. It was a ruse, and we—correction *they*—fell for it. Our fate is sealed, you see. Where did you come from?"

The young man answers, "From the east where the uprising began. I rallied the people of my district to fight the movement, but we were overpowered by the ministries—or as you put it, the Calumets—and their prolific scare tactics. We abandoned our efforts at the market square and made it to the mountains. If I were a betting man, I would wager that many of those left behind are in the camps as well. Tell me about your son."

She looks up at the young man with a stare of disorientation and bewilderment, looking closer into his face. "There will be more time for that, but first, I am interested in knowing more about you. What is your name, son?"

"I am Chanokh from Roulerville."

"Chanokh?" whispers the woman.

"Yes, my name is Chanokh, and I am from the east district of Bidonville. I traveled to Roulerville to lead the revolution. Our region was the first to fall under the law." With a firm gaze on his rustic hands, he folds them into a clenched fist and shifts his stare to the brownish-red dirt. "As the old proverb puts it, the water stone sheltered by the refreshing stream cannot begin to comprehend the misery of the exposed stone, which under new rules imposed upon it, remains scorched and suffers alone. After long seasons of complacency, Bidonville became the exposed stone. We were forced to reckon with our own reality, and the war waged upon our districts alone. It was either life under tyranny or death as free men—such was my vow to protect the innocent."

Omi says, "An oath? Why an oath, my son?"

Chanokh points to the seal in the *Book of Wisdom and Salvation* in his black and brown sack. Omi nods in acknowledgment, and they resume the conversation.

Hours later, the panoramic vista above the foggy night signals time for rest. Their faces, fading into the closure of the lightening sky, sparkle from the camp's small fire. Both the light effects and their dialogue soon draw to a close.

"Tonight, this stone will be our pillow. May the Most High's peace be with you," says Chanokh.

"Good night, my son," replies Omi.

Chanokh responds, "Peace and provisions be with you, madam."

Omi replies, "Call me Na'Omi."

Chanokh obliges and adjusts his head on the large river rock.

The following morning, the group is awakened by a light spray of a morning rain drizzling upon the bending palm branches and the algae-covered tree they slept under. The slow rippling river brightens with the opening sky. Each ripple dwindles as the gentle drops calm to a stop, bringing into view the green canopy waving its branches above.

Others begin to gather at the river to draw water. An assembly of mothers starts feeding their children morsels of bread from their sacks, and a few men round up to collect stones to form a bridge across the river. One of them staggers twelve stones in the center to link to the opposite side. Appealing to fruit dangling inconveniently above a mossy pit, others carefully hurl small pebbles at the tree.

"God has seen us well, Omi. We are still free."

Omi smiles.

"How was your sleep?" Chanokh picks up a few pebbles and playfully rattles them in his palm.

Omi brushes her gray hair from her face. "I rested, but I was frequently awakened by visions of rivers colliding and flooding towns. Aged women like me were pulled out of their beds by a deluge that cascaded from a broken mountain."

A monarch butterfly lands on a pedal behind them, and more butterflies appear, falling on the morning dew.

Omi takes notice of the colorful wings on delicate flowers. "Such peace and tranquility, but yet heaviness too, under the danger we faced. We were just below the mountains. I was escaping from the broken ground on a narrow bridge, narrowing and narrowing as the water closed in. I saw dark faces of submerged men reaching out of the murky water for my hand, but I was too far above the crossing to help them. I reached for some, but their grips weren't firm enough. They slipped from my grasp and fell to their deaths. Then the great shake opened up the ground. It swallowed them like heavy stones landing on wet paper. I stood there, amazed and troubled, staring at the cracks in the ground. All of a sudden, I began to hear whispers and voices. They were rapidly calculating numbers, and they stopped. The many voices became one. It was then I understood. Omi places her hand across her chest. "Oh, my soul. Perhaps they were the first to be rounded. Maybe that's what I saw in my dream. The ones no one was willing to stand up for. Did I mention that, in my vision, I asked the voices why this had happened?"

Chanokh replies, "No, madam."

"The voice replied sinisterly that they were calculating numbers of the age, a recurrence of every twenty-six thousand years. Chanokh, my son, do you believe we are in the last age—or has it been miscalculated?"

Chanokh looks up above to restless leaves in the trees and then to the sky.

Their attention is overtaken by an approaching buzzing sound. A distant waterfall drowns out the sound, making it difficult to identify it.

Chanokh takes hold of Omi's elbow and encourages her to take up her belongings.

Everyone else begins to stare upward, wondering where the sound is coming from. It is hard to tell, but the waving treetops give them a clue. They run in the opposite direction.

A small boy in mended rags wraps both arms tightly around his mother's neck as she bends down with the other crouching women. A chilling whirlwind whistles by, flapping the wet branches hanging above their wooly hair. The birds stop chirping, and the river stands still. The sound covers the camp.

Chanokh takes a commanding stand, shielding Omi and focusing on the women on the bank. "Get the women and children away from the river." Standing ahead of the huddle, he surveys their surroundings and observes swaying branches throughout. "Run!" Chanokh waves his arms frantically at the other men. "Run ... run deeper. Run to a high place."

Without delay, everyone scatters. With the taste of fear filling their mouths, they run from the rumblings, which beat faster as they make their way into the forest. Heat from the aircraft hastens the sweat on their backs as they run over mossy humps in the woods. Gasping for much-needed air, they run as fast as their legs will carry them. Many of the pursued wearily disappear behind the fullness of the trees, unbeknownst to the pursuers, but some try to catch up.

The raiders descend with sophisticated weapons and robots and engage the hidden mountains.

A commander raises a fist in the air to silently signal his men to stop. Pointing one group to the left and the other to the right, he leads them deeper into the forest. "They can only run so far."

One of the men closest to him is holding back a raging pack of armored and robotic dogs. The lights of the sky seem to close in, and the stars following the unfolding of another raid.

CHAPTER
EIGHT

◆◆◆

Country Life

Many years later, Folium remains resilient. The ministries' strategic maneuvers have gained ground so much so that they have instituted satellite offices in each district. They monitor every gathering in every school and in every home. The almanacs were discontinued and replaced by comedic drawings with riddles and games.

Activities from the Order of Magma appeared almost inactive compared to the acts orchestrated by Order of Exiled Kings, loyalists to the mysteries of the eastern districts. They grew very public and dominant, influencing the policies and actions of the ministries. The revolution remained abated in its attempt to overthrow the ruling bodies of the republic. Their resolve appeared almost dead except in the remote parts of the districts.

In the capital of a reformed Folium, a broadcast radio hits the airwaves with the afternoon news, followed by a requested song: "Hide Me Now under Your Wings." It is interrupted with the midday broadcast. A gray monotone voice speaks in old-fashioned French, overlaid with colonial melodies with each pause. The announcer lists the laureates of the prestigious and not-so-feted secondary schools of the hills and a few from Roulerville, Slogtown, Bidonville, and even Boucherville who managed to send their members to the underfunded and overcrowded classrooms of academia.

In the city, laureates plug their ears into the speakers. Some sit among family and pace in their fully furnished villas, and others sit on hot cement doorsteps and listen for their names to be called as the suspenseful announcement continues. The National Cathedral tolls ring at the head of the hour as pedestrians move about the square. In the center, large speakers exclaim the broadcast.

Miles away from the capital, the roll call falls on staticky speakers nailed to acacia trees. Children play in what is often dubbed as *La Cour Poussiéreuse* or dusty yard, jaunting over makeshift soccer goals and scattering chickens to make their way to the passing sugarcane vendors who sell smaller stumps to children who cannot pay for a full stalk. They race to the opposite street with defaced coins in hand, chanting philosophical phrases about sugar and the slaves whose blood cultivated the very wealth crop they harvested, a concept the children didn't really understand.

Older men play stalemate under the umbrellas of coconut trees, casting their naiveté into the wind without a premise or absolute conversational value in what they are saying. They group into clusters of other children, shoving over who's first in line for sweets. With innocence in their eyes and inexpensive sugarcane for the taking, they hum to the radio and make way to the dusty yard.

An elder emerges from his compound and observes the children playing. He calls to one of the children.

The boy quickly runs to the elder.

The elder hands him a small book. "Do you know how to read, my son?"

The boy replies, "Very little, sir."

"Tell your father to send you to my study in the morning. I will teach you how to read. I see promise in you—the potential to become a wise leader in our district."

The boy's eyes swell up as large marbles, and he slowly nods in agreement. "May Jehovah's peace be with you, Son. Go now and play. Tomorrow you will occupy your time learning the ways of a different game. Tomorrow, if God wills it, you will be groomed to become an Inkosi!"

The little Inkosi-to-be leaves the soccer game and runs home with the small book under his arms.

Jacqueline's Hometown

Miles outside the district, over the Twin Mountains, the calm of morning settles.

A round-faced, dark-skinned woman shouts, "Jacqueline!" Standing at the rear of a modest tin-roofed house surrounded by green tropical plants and long hanging clotheslines, the woman impatiently waits for a response. "Jacqueline, Oh!"

The old hut did not stand out much from the other homes in the area except for its chalky, light blue finish. The neighborhood children never called her by her proper name, Alabeau. They called her "Ma' beau" because of her coconut and vanilla cream shakes and peanut cookie chunks.

Alabeau waves her plump arms, fashioning for a quick response from Jacqueline, her demure daughter. Alabeau, one of the daughters of Malabo Bubis, moved near the banana plantations after satisfying her land pledge through proceeds of sales in the capital markets.

A rusty sign is affixed to a narrow tree in the yard, waving with the intermittent swish of wind: "Soups and Stones and Delights." It serves as a reminder to never again bet against her wages with unknown travelers. Her limited ability to read made her a perfect candidate for conniving transient merchants who offered her an opportunity to expand her small business. The conditional goodwill was that she first had to pledge her land.

Alabeau, full of excitement and never considering trickery at play, ran to her husband, an apiarist of Primorsky bees, with the uplifting proposition.

"Ma Si-beau," he said. "My love. You are a resourceful woman, indeed. I must caution you, however, to consider the motives of these visitors. Are they here to invest—or are they here to rob you of your land?"

She replied, "My gentle husband, you must not worry. I know what I am doing."

He learned from his experiences throughout the years that the same events rarely happen the same way twice. It takes a watchful eye to see things for what they really are. Having never attended school or studied the history of the Greeks and their capture of Troy, he learned the art of infiltration by studying his bees. He has the patience of an ant surgeon who examines the insides of the proverbial ant's belly by learning her ways, her habits, and her tendencies. Many summers ago, he lost his indigenous bees to the hybrid bees because he could not tell the difference between the two breeds. He was sold hybrid bees by a traveling merchant from the northern districts. The new bees, bearing a resemblance to his native queen bees, coexisted and were allowed to cohabitate the hives. *It's the nature of the bees*, he reasoned.

He later discovered that the hybrids had infiltrated the beehives by laying eggs that matured into devastating parasitic creatures, killing off the host colonies and some of his livestock. "Si-beau, be careful because some things are not what they seem."

The lesson had not made an impression on Alabeau well enough, and she suffered the consequences of a hasty and unguarded decision. She nearly lost everything, but she prevented the loss of her children to indigent servitude as was customary to unresolved debt. She had compassion for her children and never allowed them to suffer her despite her poor business decision. She was credited by her neighbors for not behaving like an ostrich that lays her eggs in a shallow ground at risk of becoming trampled on or eaten by the wilds of Folium.

"Where is your brother, Jacqueline?" Alabeau squints into the partially clouded sun with her forearm over her brow. "I ... I ... do not ... ah." Jacqueline's speech impediment is worsened by the worry in her mother's tone.

She places the dusty bottles she was reconditioning on the uneven ground and approaches her mother. Holding the hem of her tattered dress, she briskly wipes her hands. Jacqueline's brother Jacob sells kites and toys crafted from recycled canisters in the market square. He learned how to twist wires from broken radios into the tiny holes he punctured beneath wooden shoeshine boxes he found near Marche Noir. Creativity is on his side, and with meager means sufficient to produce toys for other deprived children in the area, he scrapes what he can to help support his family.

It is beginning to rain, and Alabeau is worried. The leaking roof is in dire need of repair, and the fractured white chipped enamel bucket echoes each drip; a drip for every minute she lurks for her missing son, Jacob. The steady trickle of rain splatters on the earthy floor, drizzling down to the fire, barely heating the scarred iron pot of boiling cashews. Tap and splatter after rapid taps eventually extinguish the fire. The rain intensifies with the hollowing wind, blowing away the aroma of hot roasting peanuts and the cacao plants drying on the mahogany racks. They are soon replaced by the scent of damp red clay.

Jacqueline's shoulder is weighed down as she nervously waits for her brother's return. "Sh … sh, should I … I … I go search for …" She slams her hand on the pruning but is quickly interrupted by her mother.

"No. Let's wait for just a little longer. He and Marc could be returning from the tourist port or the market!"

Marc, a shoeshine boy, typically follows Jacob to the market. They are often seen together throughout the town as partners in commerce. Alabeau sits down for a moment, ponders for a bit longer, and slowly stands. Her late husband's faded picture unevenly hangs next to the makeshift dinner table. She tightens her waist with a birth cloth and runs outside, covering her hair with what is left of Jacob's school uniform. He hadn't worn it since the family could no longer afford government-subsidized tuition. Leaping over puddles like a toddler making her way to a steady wall trying to prevent a tumble, she bounces between huts and quivering trees to one of the larger and sturdier trees. She rests under the giant tree facing the main road. "Jacob!" she shouts.

The wind intensifies with and fans away any real hope of Jacob's return. She cries out louder, again and again, bracing her bosom as she did thirteen years ago when nursing her son while her husband traveled to the city to search for a better life for the family. "Jacob!" she wails again.

No one answers—only the howl of the wind.

Back at home, Jacqueline races for buckets and cooking pots to capture the rainwater dancing on the dirt floor. Hours pass as darkness covers the sky, occasionally sparked by lightning. Jacqueline pauses from her flood-control task and calls out, "Maman!" She hears no answer. "Ma … Ma … Maman!" She tries to find her mother, but she only hears tree branches crackling and more rain. She runs outside in search for her mother, but Alabeau is nowhere to be found. Jacqueline solemnly reenters the house, talking to herself to cope with the situation. The storm intensifies throughout the hour with loud thunder and torrential rain, but there is still no mother or brother in sight. Jacqueline screams and covers her ears as a large tree falls with its far-reaching branches loudly brushing against the outside walls, nearly damaging the already fragile roof. Ironically, the tree serves as a protective barrier from the oncoming rain and redirects the downpour to a slope on the roof.

Finally, after hours of cold rain, Alabeau emerges from the crossroad, wet and desolate. Jacqueline runs to her mother with both arms open wide and covers her with a partially dry rag that was suspended on the door's hinge.

The next morning, shreds of dried palm leaves litter the provincial ruins, plastered on faded political billboards of slogans about rehabilitation and timeworn promises. As her mother controls her tickling cough, she looks into Jacqueline's brown eyes and cracks a small smile.

Jacqueline tries to utter words, but her mother places her finger over her lips and shushes her. "It's okay, my dear."

They casually clean up around their waterlogged home. "Do you think Jacob is okay, ma … ma … ah … ah … now that the rain has … stopped?"

Her mother points to the sky and replies, "God is great and will protect him, my child."

Not a moment too soon, a swaying shadow emerges from the muddy road. It resembles Jacob's distinct walk. As the silhouette approaches the light, he is immediately recognized. With slumped shoulders and carrying his wet shoes, he reluctantly approaches his mother and sister,. "I am sorry."

Alabeau and Jacqueline run and hug him, nearly knocking him over.

"Where have you been?" Alabeau asks. He tells them of his newfound employment and the inability to leave because of the sudden rainstorm. He is hushed and embraced by Alabeau and Jacqueline. This delicate near miss reminds Alabeau of her husband's tragic disappearance, and she is gentle with her son.

As it turns out, Jacob's absence was brought about by his recent employment with the Pluton Emplacement. While there, he served as a part-time helper to the manuscript keeper. He was tasked with stocking shipments in the storage building and recording inventory. His other assignment was transporting supplies from the stores to the square. His slim frame supported half the weight carried by his older counterparts, but he had relentless energy that kept him employed. In the afternoon, during teatime, outside of the closed doors, he would hear prominent men discussing politics, war, economics and philosophical concepts that were well above his level of interest—except on occasions when *harvest* or *revolution* caused emotions to rise.

"If it weren't for the men there, I could not have possibly received this work," Jacob says.

"What men?" Alabeau asks.

He puts down his cup of hot tea. "Mama, you should have seen them. They were important men with superior shoes and bowties and coats like the ones worn by the ministries. Mr. Amram, who was probably the boss, said, 'Boy, come here.' I put down my shoeshine box and came to him. 'Do you know how to count, boy?' Count what? I thought to myself."

Jacqueline laughs and covers her mouth to control her giggle.

"'Yes, mister. I know how to count, sir,' I replied. Mr. Amram walked over to me, handed me a book, and pointed me to a huge garage or storage place. Other boys like me were lifting and caring and moving about and just doing work. Mama, I accepted the job right there on the spot." Jacob picks up the tea mug and takes a small sip. "Umm, it's still hot." He puts it down and looks at his sister. "Jacqui, he called us little Inkosis. How unusual. Don't you think?"

She replies, "Mmm."

Alabeau asks, "My son, why didn't you come home sooner? I was worried sick, standing there in the middle of the cold rain, having it slapping me and shaking me about like a fish in the sea. I could have lost my mind on those flooded streets if wasn't for the baker who came outside after hearing me calling your name. Jacqueline, remind me to send Mr. Guangzhou two bags filled with twisted warps of chocolate chunks, roasted cashews, sweet potatoes, sliced lam veritab, and a large bottle of goat milk—not from the spotted one but the loud one that bleats all the time. I said I would tie him near the chickens. Maybe that would help control his nerves."

Jacob is still shivering under a blanket.

Joyfully clapping her hands, Alabeau asks, "So, my boy has found work. Tell me, my child, how much do they pay—and why did he call you an Inkosis? Is it some type of game?"

"Maman, the boss man said he sees potential in me to be a leader and the pay, well, it is according to the number of deliveries I make. Mother, I was given a vest too. It reads: P-P-P."

Alabeau says, "Never mind that now. Son, drink your tea. We are having cocoa tonight. I am boiling the chocolate blocks now. Jacqueline, fetch me some bread underneath that cloth in that basket. And please close the hatch, will you? The wind is coming in and jumbling the mist with the fire." She begins to hum a familiar tune. "Tomorrow, we are going to pick some corn for the harvest."

The cocoa oil rumbles in the boiling pot, sending sweet fumes through the cracks in the roof.

Alabeau calmly says, "Jacqueline, sweetheart, bring me the peanuts."

"Yes, Mother. I wonder what this harvest will bring."

Alabeau replies, "Only time will tell, dear. Only time will tell." The pot continues to boil, and Alabeau continues humming.

CHAPTER
NINE

◆◆◆

The Raid

The eighteen hundredth harvest is approaching, and plans are underway for a monumental celebration. In Bidonville, however, they are contending with a quasi-state of siege that begins and ends almost cyclically. The people are living in a constant state of angst but look forward to the harvest as a form of escaping from the reality of life. The ministries continue to promise the people of Folium that change is coming, but they reintroduce and recycle the same policies. As problem-solution reaction, it is commonplace to have men from outside districts providing security in the squares during the harvest, although they have no loyalty or accountability to the people. The populace becomes almost paralyzed in local protests and begins to accept this as the fate of their district and have given up the pursuit for a revolution.

It is getting later, and the cathedral bell tolls. It slightly echoes from the villages near the shores to the hills, but this time is different. The birds are flying in the opposite direction and out of formation. The dogs begin to whimper and bark, but only if dogs could speak. The stories they would tell and warnings they would share. Sadly, they are unable to alert their masters about what is about to come. Those living closest to the shores watch as large ships remain stationary at the disappearing horizon. Like large stones emerging out of the sea, their presence is intimidating.

Bidonville is not at ease. An impending danger in the air can be felt by many, humming with an unnerving deathly silence. An eerie calm descends boulevards and crossroads, closer with every hour and every toll. Children in front of the La Place fearfully run to their homes as the men patrolling the cobblestone streets arrived earlier than expected. They methodically approach the square. Precision in each step, they tread in and out of side streets, searching for alleged bandits. While hiding out in open courtyards and dusty alleys, they assume their positions.

Considered by town dwellers as meandering vipers who strike in the shadows of their handlers with unchallenged authority, the raiders shrouded in their conspicuous garb—helmets and shoulder patches—operate in anonymity. They pour out into the streets of Bidonville, strategically scattered in regimented form. Grimaced faces behind monotone uniforms run beside passing tanks with rifles erected. This ridiculously unnecessary exercise puts doubt in the hearts of the dwellers as they watch the rifles leading the way of marching men and envoys of camouflage trucks. They begin to realize that it is not a drill or routine. It is an actual raid.

At the eleventh hour, when evening Mass had already ended and presumed silence had reached its peak, horsepower roars past elevated entry gates, bronze cathedral bells, and the vacant central square. The wet stones beneath lithesome boots part into splats, like the raindrop falling into a half-filled enamel bucket placed beneath a peasant's leaking roof, dancing in spirals until it overflows into a flood. The rapid taps quickly accelerate into a storm in Bidonville's square. Alongside gray metallic tank, guns reflecting the moonlight glare, akin to elephant trunks pointing at a dark sub-Saharan sky, they march on. Hunched men scramble across dimmed light posts and pillars, waiting for their next orders. It is almost invisible to anyone peeking through the cracks of a window, but it is fluid enough to establish that Bidonville is under full siege and that orders had been given to engage any moving target without prejudice.

A loud boom is heard blocks away from where the men positioned their artillery, in the direction of the ministry of affairs building, not too far from the port of customs. In a single shot, Bidonville is suddenly undressed, exposed of her vulnerability and tattered veils of a sanctuary. It is evident that this is not a drill.

The Calumets

Beyond the dark streets, Reimonde Moyenne—the sixth generation of Rimon—a local civil engineer situated at the foot of the hills of Roulerville, miles from the shantytown, is awakened from his light slumber by the rumbling below. Veering inconspicuously into his barred Victorian window and between unpainted Greco columns to take a precocious view, he rations his thoughts to no provocation. The status quo is at play. It could be the electoral ruckus from the masses since it was not uncommon and seemingly was limited to the square. Curiosity, however, brings him to study the developing theater from afar with suspicion. At such a span, he is safe and not at risk, but this does not calm his nerves. His warm breath deflects on the gradually fogging window and blurs his vision. Pressing firmly to see better, as though becoming one with the ivory veneer, he gawks with rapid eyes following along as the events develop.

Reimonde whispers, "Dear Lord, save the people of Bidonville." His inner prayer is muzzled by the unnerving beating in his chest and in his thoughts, bringing up fears from the past that he dreaded in his imagination. His faith, family, and homeland were critical pieces in a game of chess where the kings are hidden from view, and he is the sensible rook who is ineffective in the grand scheme of things, but neutral to both players. After all his rationalization and politics sit idle and inactive, he thinks outside himself. His saving grace has always been his faith, but his social understanding was underwritten by his colonial education, softening his resolve. Time has seen this sort of thing before, and chaos was inevitable. Social strife was the mainstay of his district's history, and it did not seem to be changing anytime soon—not in his lifetime. This struggle, this game, is like a complicated game of chess where the moving hand is never seen and only hinted at in books.

His father had said, "My son, there is never a stalemate in an active game."

"Then what do you suggest is an active game, Papa, because the game is over by then, right?" asked Reimonde.

"Walk with me, my son," his father replied as they proceeded to the private garden overlooking his study. "A game is active as long as those who control the pieces remain hidden, apart from the players and nonexistent to the pawns. Do you understand, my son?"

Reimonde responded, "Not with certainty, Papa. Who's hidden—and what sort of rules are these?"

His father replied, "Son, the pieces are always moving in an active game."

"Yes, Papa," Reimonde replied. "Therefore, to remain as such, someone has to be playing, but in this case, the engaging player has higher players dictating and controlling the moves behind him. His opponent never sees these players and will not know what hit him."

"Well, who are the players—the ones who are dictating the moves?"

His father grinned. "You decide. You decide when it's your move. You can decide to become the opposition or enter the game as the lower player where you are no more than a pawn of the oppressors."

His father's voice fades in his mind. His gaze begins to blur into a compilation of rambling thoughts and fear. Although he is acutely aware of the repercussion of the emotion, he wrestles with its effects and draws his attention back to a focus, pivoting toward his family in the great room. "Madine, you can tell when the helmets are coming. You can smell the fuming diesel in the air and distinct rattling as their trucks turn into the corridor and make their way to the Carrefour. These men are known for raiding shanties at night. The raiders! The Calumets!"

Rubbing his sweaty brow, he points to the rear halls. "It's best that we secure the front and side gates and remain indoors tonight. Certainly, it's safer here in the back of the house." He gestures toward the small living quarters, covered by overgrown hibiscus and argun palms." They hastily go down through the foyer and around to the rear of the two-story house, holding hands in the dark and careful not to alert anyone of their brisk escape.

"Jacqueline will be arriving in the morning to wash the stewpots. The debacle will be over by morning, undoubtedly. I am sure the barricades between the market crossroads will delay her. We can settle our stead here throughout the night and maybe into the morning break."

As he turns for his wife's acknowledgment, he unintentionally kicks a dented marble decorated with red, blue, and fading black stripes. His patriotic gem rolls down the smooth floor, vanishes into the kerosene-lit room, and rests against a chipped white enamel bucket under the maid's cot, adjacent to the modestly finished kitchen.

Thus far, the only sound in the darkened kitchen functions as a ringing gong to an impending event or a prelude to a symphony of gloom, fading into a backdrop of rapid scrambling rubber boots, corded with sounds of barking dogs and crumbling sidewalk pavements.

Tucked into a dark corner where only the tips of their nose are visible to one another,

Reimonde whispers, "Madine?"

"Reimonde?"

"Are you there, Madine?"

"Yes. Yes, I am … I mean … we are all here." The cadence of their hearts is drumming in unison as she places one hand on her chest and another on her husband's. Heavy breathing and whispers blend together in a dreadful reminder of the past. "The raiders are here! The raiders are here! The raiders are here!"

Reimonde says, "Madine, listen to me—and don't say no to what I am about to tell you. If they find us here, I want you to—"

"No!" Madine exclaims. "Don't speak like this, my darling. I am not going to run away while you stay here alone to be killed." She looks into his eyes and tearfully begs him to reconsider his plan. She rubs his warm cheeks and kisses him tightly not wanting to let go in what is becoming a horrific darkening night. Notwithstanding the painful reality of death if they stay and the wrenching pain tugging at her stomach, she continues to hold on.

"Madine, listen to me, sweetheart. These men, if the rumors are true—and I believe them to be so—can do awful things. They are not even nationals and have no loyalty or love for our people. What do they care for us? We mean nothing to them—nothing at all. Promises made and broken is the same rubbish we have been fed over these years, which is why we never saw this coming."

In a manic state of paranoia, he places his hands on his head, pulls his wife closer, and begins to pray with her. Overhead, chopping blades whisk past the hills and down to the center point, thrusting hoary dust into makeshift doorways and leaving them naked and unbarred. The bones of the city rattle, unable to reason or plead. It is sure that tonight's verdict is imminent and perhaps, for many, fatal. Bidonville is ransacked and tossed into turmoil throughout the early hours.

The dreadful resonance comes to an abrupt stop, but within moments, it is overtaken by the howls of nervous mutts and hysterical people running to and fro. Parting echoes of screams, daunting screams, and searing bullets clamber on metal rooftops and shattering doorsteps. Rifle butts make entry, and machetes follow. If it were not in the city, one would have mistaken each strike as men threshing sugarcane stalks, making their way into the ripening crop.

The air plagues with a reemergence of imported arms that indiscriminately fire at will. Barred doors are incapable of suiting their purpose, and refuge cannot be found behind any wall.

Even the ones shielding the eyes of crouching children, who bunged tightly with hopes of shrouding themselves from the boogiemen running amok outside or perhaps from the incessant wails piercing the frightening night.

Reimonde has a flashback of his childhood and hears his father words at the justice assembly.

Continuum has never seen such brutality in recent history. Her earth cries out with the voices of her people and is heard by diasporas and humanitarians at heart. Some sit before imported wine bottles to discuss solutions and end with none at all, just another social event with ineffectual programs. Several delegates of many districts are sent to appeal to the ministry of justice and her proxy agencies, among them clergymen from select regions. Following the harvest, the assembly is broadcast over the national radio.

An announcer begins to speak at the end of introductory music. "People of Folium, we bring you a rebroadcast of the recent assembly by the ministry of justice."

Elder Moyenne approaches the podium and introduces himself.

Reimonde runs to his mother and interrupts her conversation with one of the housemaids. "*Maman, venez vite. Il est temps d'ecouter.* It's eleven o'clock. Come … come, Maman. Papa is about to speak."

Madame Moyenne puts down pieces of imported fabrics and joins little Reimonde in the great room near the large radio. The medium of choice refuses to tell lies to their vision.

Holding on her arm, Reimonde smiles. "His speech is next, Maman."

A voice forcefully comes through the speaker, saying, "In the name of the Most High, Jehovah God, the Magnificent and Merciful, I greet you. May the peace of God be with you! Director of the board, delegates, and members of the council, it is an honor that you would agree to hear me speak today and present the plea of my people and sentiments from my own heart." Elder Moyenne begins to passionately paint a picture of a nation that has declined from greatness to days of famine and war, further graven by the raiders of their land who drive millions to flee to neighboring districts on foot. He speaks of his dissonance with the inaction on the part of Slogtown and his own district.

"Gentlemen of the ministry of justice, members of the global council, and executors of the art of casuistry and sophistry, I come to you as a humble servant of the people and a voice for the voiceless. Today, I speak to you of an epidemic of a great proportion that you and everyone else in this room are keenly aware of. Such evil, should it be allowed to prevail unadulterated, will eventually overwhelm the consciousness of those who remain and doubtfully create a nation of madmen. The dark matter your leaders authorized to remain free, fully charged, and unabated will only continue to grow. It will become a resourceful tool for those who would see it fit to depopulate a nation of innocent people further than we have seen in our time. I don't see a way out of this situation with the options such as the ones the ministries presented to the gentleman of the West District. These revolting and dreadful acts epitomize the worst of humanity and will destroy us from within. I am filled with indignation when I remember the stories reported of the dismemberment and the ungodly and cruel termination of life in the southern borders in the eye of a crying continent. Nearly eight hundred thousand lives have been viciously snatched from existence, gentlemen. That is what the officials have been able to account, but I am sure there are more. I can only conclude by these figures that, as a nation, we permitted genocide. I submit to you today that if Folium could die from the shame of indifference, she would have died a thousand deaths by now. Therefore, my goal today is not to present facts to lure you into a state of shame. I am here today to speak to the world in this forum, and before God as my witness—"

The director says, "Mr. Moyenne, what do you propose we should have done? Send our men into kill zones to appease the sentiments of the press and the citizens of Folium? Eh? I will not have that on my conscience. I trust neither would you or any reasonable person in our position."

Elder Moyenne replies, "No, Director. I am not saying that you make a political gesture. I am acutely aware of the stakes. I am saying that war had been declared on humanity, and an independently elected body and the nations it represents did nothing."

A brief silence is heard. Little Reimonde gets up to check the connection and then hears his father again. "I am sorry, gentlemen. Allow me a moment to regain myself."

He says, "All throughout Continuum, we are afforded the opportunity to right the wrongs we have committed by presenting them before the Almighty and Most High God, but the people of Folium refuse to repent. They have placed the next generation in a challenging predicament, perpetuating the curse coming upon the nations. Will this body become complicit in the undoing of the blessings we have come to enjoy?

The director replies, "Then what are you arguing that the ministry do? You accuse this bureau of treasonous acts and offer no solution. Continuum is filled with thousands of dead gods, Mr. Moyenne, who have failed to prove their usefulness at any moment in our history. You must understand that our history is written with violence. It is the nature of man. We cannot govern the actions of man. We can only mitigate the impacts to our people and interests. This is not a forum to hear about your beliefs and accusations of despotic actions."

Elder Moyenne replies, "The diaspora, sons and daughters of Freeland, have already proven to Folium and the entire world the degree to which she is inept and unable to protect her people, and now she further proves that point in her inability to send aid to her brothers and sisters who are falling at the sword because of their faith. I have already spoken to my people at length on this matter, but I understand that they are victims of an empire themselves, enslaved to ideologies that keep them busy with meaningless things. My purpose here today, above all, is to task you with a new role in challenging your leaders and member districts to repent and change your humanitarian policies. Ladies and Gentlemen of this assembly, I tell you this. If you allow this evil to continue to incubate into a form of policy for the execution of undesirables and enemies of whatsoever, its tentacles will grow beyond that border, and it will seep into the coast of Folium and someday rise to fly at your throat. That evil, this unimaginable evil, will spiral back to strangle you and your children in a far and distant future after you have already forgotten and become complacent, resting peacefully in your beds as presumably free men. You will call upon your dead gods, as you put it, Mr. Director, but they will not hear your supplication. History has made it clear and evident to those who would learn from her classroom that justice delayed is no solution at all. Evil nurtured anywhere is a pass for more evil everywhere else. I serve a just God, a living and relevant God. A loving God, but one that judges with a fiery sword, and with these words, I warn Folium that judgment is coming—if not in your lifetime, but someday. Whether by ruckus or silently, a revolution is coming, and with this member of this body, I bid you the best of outcomes."

Madine sobs and says, "Ray, come, dear, you mustn't stand there so close to the window. It is much too dangerous over there." She waves her needle-pricked fingers and arches her back.

Reimonde says, "This is no place for an expectant mother, Madine! No place …"

Madine's near-term labor and elevated glucose make her ill fit for sudden movement or agitation. She rests her head on a small red pillow.

The sky echoes from below, illuminated by flickering fire. Suddenly, an ominous hum can be heard outside, but shortly after, they hear rapid fire of automatic weapons.

Crackling effects of burning shanties and modest homes draws the bombardment closer from the poorest and unseen to nearby towns, lending themselves to clouds of obscurity moving upward with the western winds, toward the hills, and then cascading down over the national police headquarters and its fluttering red and blue flags, above open courtyards and between the narrows of alleys.

Reimonde, feeling like a capon barred by twisted wires established to protect him, is now melancholy. Reimonde, as a testament, is isolated by class, but affected nonetheless, in a powerless personal state of siege. He resigns from his post and joins his family, head hung low, tapping his foot on the cement floor, attempting to conjure logical ideas. Reimonde begins to shake.

In emotional agony, he urges his wife and daughter to stay down. With a tremor in his voice and then with certainty, he shouts, "Madine, they are calling for heavier artillery! They are fervently making their way up the hills, Madine! Madine!" The situation is full of dread in the direst state.

Impeded by the rising haze from below, the Moyennes anxiously scramble for a safer part of the maid's quarters to hide, but the small space can barely accommodate them. Nearby, rapid footsteps scatter into houses, and window shutters slam shut. Waiting like prisoners chained together in a cave, they brace themselves as moving shadows and sounds of heavy machinery pass by. One of the unknown shadows outside stops and towers over the trees. Slowly moving across the neighboring wall, the family's fear intensifies. The shadow stops and remains motionless as if it has spotted its victim. Their imagination conjures the worst possibility of what is to come. It is too much for them to bear, and crying out for mercy at this stage might be premature. They hear forceful entries into houses nearby and women screaming in the streets. For certain, these raiders are killing people—and won't spare women and children. They whisper a prayer for protection and for God's eyes to see them in the dark room.

Meanwhile, in the shantytowns below, the attacks shift and are met with insurrection. An uproar of a moving mob makes an impression by smashing the heads of iconic monuments. They are joining in the raid for personal advantage out of the chaos, and they are not being stopped by the raiders. It's as though they are working for the same people. In the streets, uniformed men blend in with organized street ruffians for pillaging.

The Moyennes remain still, listening to their heartbeats. "The raiders are here! The raiders are here! The raiders are here!"

Moments pass from minutes to hours of exhaustion and steady suspense well into the break of morning. At last, the sun lends its light to twisting shades of gray, hot haze, and solemn assurance. The Moyennes' circumstance is short of a fatal verdict. They survived, but they are broken emotionally, traumatized with other families scattered at the foot of the hills.

Three days later, the Moyennes receive their newborn son, Raymond VII, with the help of midwives and parishioners of the nearby church. Holding his swaddled son while gazing into his brown eyes, Reimonde sings, "Hide me now, under your wings." With tears rolling from Reimonde's eyes, he looks up. "Cover me within your mighty hand." The couple returns home days later. Standing in their front yard, they survey the grounds for potential damage, carefully walking over their small entry garden, which is littered with debris from a hectic night of rioting.

The following week, Reimonde returns with his wife and newborn son to the Iconium—not as a habitual parishioner, but as a voice to the unspoken words long remained so because of the complacency of the temple body.

Entering the elder's chamber with his son in his arms and his wife to his left, his mind is fixed on the week's unfolding events and undeterred by the conversations around him. The day has been graciously arranged by the temple elders after he expressed the egregious events the week before and how the Most High moved him to speak to the people.

One of the elders from the southern region approaches Reimonde and places his right hand on Reimonde's right shoulder.

"Ah, Baba. Your son is a great gift from the Eternal to you and your family—and to our people an even preeminent gift. In time, he will learn of the hidden kingdom and the multitude watching and waiting to see if he will complete his mission and finally be crowned as one of the many great kings of our land."

"A king, you say?" questions Reimonde.

The elder points to the northern part of the sky. "As many before, chosen by the Most High to fulfill his promise. Your father's father knew this and traveled for wisdom and came to the point of revelation. Your son must do the same. You must train him in the way he should go. When he is old, he will not depart from it. As king, he will serve the King of Kings of the mysterious kingdom of God."

Reimonde is grieved with the awesome responsibility presented by the elder and reflects for a moment, and when it appears that he has regained his focus and returned to the topic, the elder says, "You have a future king in your care, an Inkosis, but he has before him two paths: the liberation of our people if he fulfills the commission or a partaker of the cyclical curse if he fails."

Reimonde thanks the elder, and others begin to approach him with similar sentiments.

"The service will start shortly, and the hour is short. You must speak truth, love, and the name of our Lord incarnate: Yeshua Hamashiac."

Reimonde kisses his son's forehead, hands him over to his wife, and proceeds to exit the room for the entry hall.

After the choir joyfully completed the lead-in song and cleared the pulpit, Reimonde approaches the platform, rests the *Book of Wisdom and Salvation* on the stand, and clears his throat before addressing the congregation. "In the name of the Jehovah and in the incarnate Son, Yeshua, the merciful and benevolent God, I greet you in peace."

The congregation replies, "May his peace be with you, Brother."

Reimonde calls the congregation to prayer saying, "Elohim ... Elohim ... Elohim ... Elohim!"

The congregation replies in Latin, "We live only once, but you live forever. The alpha and the omega! Elohim ... Elohim ... Elohim ... Elohim!"

Reimonde, like his father, speaks in a rhythmic and eloquent fashion, moving the hidden passions of whoever hears him. He begins his message on the atrocities committed on the least of society and how those acts are not incidental and do not discriminate with time. He points out that evil will find its way to the hills too and in a matter of time all the corners of Continuum if the people don't wake up their minds to see it. He shifts the focus to himself and the others present, pointing out that complacency of the people is what gives full reign to evil and apathy.

"Several generations deep, and we have lost our culture, language, and true religion. If you look close enough, you'll see it—the memory of those before us compressed into lines of magma stretching deep into that rock with every year. When our time is up—and it is coming whether you are ready for it or not—it will come. When it does, we will be yet another line, possibly forgotten and dormant, but there. We are only three generations away from becoming forgotten. So, I say to you, make an impact that is timeless, lest the coming shift overcomes you by surprise like a blind man given sight only after he is placed in his coffin. What good is it to him then? I can already see the shift. Can you? This language we speak in Folium is transforming into something we can no longer recognize. Parents with children—or shall I say children with parents living in the same dwelling—speak two different languages and will soon practice two different religions."

The congregation shouts, "Teach, my brother! Teach!"

Meanwhile, a few younger members of the temple lark about outside, challenging each other on their knowledge of the latest social events and the attire they plan to wear at the next harvest. Enjoying the meaningless things of life and swelling their pride with the passing of time, they ignore the teachings and guidance of their elders.

Inside, Reimonde continues with his message, captivating a young man by named Obadiah, who reminded him of himself when he marveled at his father's words.

"How long will you remain obsolete and not see you are losing your homes to meaningless things and the system that has changed all things sacred? How long will you become irrelevant to the progression of excellence and unable to contribute time-tested truths to the next generation?"

The congregation shouts, "Teach us, brother! Teach!"

Reimonde passionately raises his voice and waves his hand with each reflection. "Such truth that must not absolve, regardless of the times and seasons must be kept alive. You must circle back around and turn from your destructive path, but you must first see where you are headed, lest you continue under this course unaware as your fathers' fathers did before. You must do this, I tell you, lest you become despised by the rest of Folium and again become slaves to the very kingdom you helped build. I am here to help you see your unabated trajectory, your patterns, and your tendencies in a world where things aren't always what they seem. Has your acquiescence allowed your cognitive abilities to fall at the end of the bell curve? I say to you all, my brothers and sisters, that regardless of your outer form—whether it be yellow, black, or white—we are all precious in his sight and have sufficient consciousness potential to understand his truth. I submit again to you these questions: Are you sleeping? Are you in a deep coma and unaware of what is happening around you. Are you another generation of imbeciles, happy and full from the trappings of the king's table, fattening up for the day of his great harvest?

"Are you keeping up—or are you following the lies to your vision? Most of you have many of them in your homes. You go to bed with one in your hands and propped up, dead-centered on your walls, and under your pillow and wake up to worship its existence. It's what Folium has given you as the hellish family altar if you choose to allow it to be so, if you so choose to consume it in the improper and polluted measure. Did not our brother remind the Greeks and we as well that my 'brothers and sisters, whatever is true, whatever is noble, whatever is right, whatever is pure, whatever is lovely, whatever is admirable—if anything is excellent or praiseworthy—think about such things'? Did he not? If you agree with these holy words, why do you continue to feed the machine starving your essence of virtue? It is because you have not changed masters? If so, I regretfully inform you that you are a slave!

"It calls upon you, and you answer it. Do you not? Its phantom glare and vibration control your every thought. From a young age, you lay your children at the altar of the beastly statue of antiquity, which has taken a new form over the generations. I am not speaking of the furnace that consumes your unwanted, unborn, and partially born, but that false light that flickers and reprograms your thoughts. Some call it the digital, and others call it the *dajjal*.

"The fabric of family ties has withered with the times, and the evidence of their new loyalties has become quite evident. One found in Folium's guild and her escaping pleasures. One where the old are cast away, and the lives of babes are optional, left to the will of their mothers and Folium's masters. Wake up! Wake up from this curse you are under. Wake up and see the invisible bars you stand behind, the prison of the mind. Wake up, you slaves! May God, help the people of Folium!

"We have become a nation of mindless subjects, living in a state of delirium. In fact, the very thought you have in your head right now is not your own. It was implanted. You forgot how to think because Folium has done it for you. You have forgotten how to think. Do you know what is happening around you? I mean right now. Who owns your mind? Do those who own it ever permit you an iota of time to your God-given mind—or is it constantly connected to that great machine that we call Folium and her vices? Claim it back, reconnect it to the kingdom of the Most High, and you will see what I see. Your eyes will be opened to truth, wisdom, and love. Take it back and be set free. Claim it back and become one collective mind under the sun and beyond. Claim it back! Can you see it for yourself—or are you just another sleeping sheep in Folium, ready to be swallowed up by Continuum's fire? A revolution is coming, I tell you. Whether silent or by a ruckus, the revolution is coming. A spiritual awakening that will reveal the lost sheep within a men and women. Now, my brothers and sisters, I am not talking about abrasive and abrupt action.

No. We don't advocate violence. As it was said in the Rhine by our brother, the French mathematician Pascal, 'Justice without power is empty, but power without justice is only violence.'

"And what about love? You have forgotten how to do that too. And to those who have, I say to you, 'Snatch it back.' Was it not written as the summation of all the laws? Did not our father teach us that, above all, love each other deeply because love covers a multitude of sins? I am not talking about eros or philistia love, but unselfish agape love. As it is said in the *Book of Wisdom and Salvation*—I am holding one in my hand—there will be many who will be lovers of themselves, lovers of money, boastful, proud, abusive, disobedient to their parents, ungrateful, unholy, without love, unforgiving, slanderous, without self-control, brutal, not lovers of the good, treacherous, rash, conceited, lovers of pleasure rather than lovers of God—having a form of godliness but denying its power. Have nothing to do with such people. I believe you can do it. Can we do it? Are you ready for the revolution?"

The congregation shouts, "Yes!"

"Do we have what it takes to do it?"

The congregation shouts, "Yes!"

"Do you have the heart and soul to climb to that high mountain of holiness? Oh yes, yes, yes. I pray that you have the collective heart to say, 'Create in me a clean heart, O God, and renew a steadfast spirit within me.' I hope and dream to see my people, his chosen people, all nations who call upon the name of the Most High, say, 'Yes, Lord, yes.'"

The congregation shouts, "Yes, Lord, yes!"

He says, "Can we do it? Can you peacefully but forcefully change this condition you find yourself in? Can your voice rise above meaningless things to the critical matters before you today? Can you relinquish the nontangible things of Folium and be a people united. Are you ready for the revolution?"

The congregation shouts, "Yes, we are ready!"

Visions of warriors battling in a celestial battlefield come to Reimonde's mind. He envisions his likeness leading the battle—evil on one side and righteousness on the other, converging into a large fire encircling the enemy. He replies, "Then, we shall do it!" Once again, he surveys the hulls of the Iconium and points to the decorated ceiling. "I tell you this that when Continuum is shaken and the stars of the lower heaven rattle, your safety will be found in the Most High. He is your dwelling place. He is the mountain you must seek. So I ask you again, are you ready?"

They reply, "Yes!"

"I said, are you ready for the revolution?"

The congregation replies louder, "Yes, yes, yes!"

"May his protection be upon you. May God bless Bidonville. May the peace of the Most High God be with you—and May he have mercy on the people of Folium." He turns his back and walks away from the pulpit.

Years later, after Reimonde's speech and subsequent community rallies, an upsurge of spiritual awareness sprang out of the desert of despair to a spiritual renaissance. Multitudes from Bidonville traveled throughout Roulerville, Slogtown, and Boucherville to lead small spiritual revolutions. The spirit of hope seemed to outshine the glitter of meaningless and ungodly things of Folium and began turning the tides to a vastness of unselfish love, germinating unrecognizable clusters of allied districts. The revolution birthed a new nation that survived all odds—until the tide changed again, ushering with it a seven-year famine.

"Famines are a created weapon to control the people. Manufactured scarcity at the hand of the ministries has made the stomach of my countrymen his new advisor," exclaims Reimonde.

During the reign of lawlessness, the ripples in the sky and underground cavities became a common occurrence. Dependency on all things customary failed every man's heart. Folium is in a tug-of-war between passionate submission to the Most High and the empty bellies of the faithful. People are beginning to consult their empty stomachs for political discernment and the state of their misery for spiritual direction. The revolutionary fire simmers into plumes of smoke, fanning away with the new ideas of the age. The revolution seems to die as quickly as it was birth, another countermove of Folium's kings.

Seven years later, in an age of jubilance, an economic shift presented the people with a hope rooted again in materialism. Folium reveals its promise made to those willing to abandon their traditional values and enrich them with substanceless bliss, making light of any talk of social change. The societal unrest and production capacity throughout the districts has increased by sevenfold. At hills of the great harvest, Folium is rising to become a greater republic than promised. While the divided factions among the districts had not receded, the empire is rising above all speculations of a default. The ministries maintain order, power, and fraternity throughout the districts—even among the exiles of the religious regions.

Mighty men rose among those reduced to meaningless things, and conversation among the masses returns to normal. The memory of the raids had been swept under the rugs. While still mentioned in school and gatherings, it wasn't personal enough to the new generation to be held as a beacon. It is now commonplace for the subjugated heralds to find themselves as idle and ineffective in their homes—with labor and even growth of the inner self. As useful fools of the great agenda, the people of Folium remain in an alpha state of awareness as they graze on the proverbial farms of the districts. Some robustly dive down without fail under a wide range of social changes by adopting repugnant ideas as a new inspiration. The stimulus they see as freedom from what they perceive to be moral captivity soon imprisons them. Reflecting the deeds from the outer worlds in alliance with Folium, they go about their days as mindless pawns in an engineered master plan.

Father and Son

Raymond is now in his preadolescence and suffering from an identity crisis, which is aggravated by the taunting he receives from his classmates. He tries to fit in with the rest of the socialites in his school, but his personality does not meet the standard. Whenever he would share his trials upheld by the hands of those he calls friends, his father says, "And we cannot subject ourselves to their subculture. Don't worry yourself with friends. I am your friend. Your mother and siblings are your friends." On this side of the milieu, those words are irrelevant. This is his world—the one he lives in day in and day out as a sojourner on the road he calls life.

After one of the family's daily devotions, Raymond retires to his room to rearrange his miniature ships he displays next to books written by renowned scholars and his father. Almost mindlessly playing with the wooden crafts, he preoccupies his mind with something other than the dark feeling of nonexistence in what his father often calls "the subculture."

These words did not have meaning and life in them. Raymond withdrew to a display of static arrangements of ships. He immediately looks to his mirror hung next to words taken out of the book he often reads during devotion and begins to weep.

His father enters the room with a hot blend of pineapple, aloe, and ginger and walks over to sit on the side of his bed. "Raymond, why do you stand there looking at your face in the mirror, hoping to find confidence? The confidence you are searching for, my son, is not in there, but in you. My son, the day you surrender your purpose and identity to others, you have already willfully given yourself to their will. You are, therefore, their slave and they your master. Do you see what I am telling you, my son?"

Wiping away the tears streaming down his cheek, he answers, "No, Papa. I don't."

His father picks on the ships and looks through the sails. "In Continuum, many have searched for meaning and value, but they come out empty-handed. Come. Come and sit near me, my boy, and allow me to show you what you cannot see standing up and what elders like me can see even while sitting down.

"In the rural parts of Folium, there was a family of young domesticated quails that were free to roam the farms they lived in. They knew nothing else but the four squares of their encampment. This is where they received their daily nourishment and care from the farmer who owned them. One day, three days before the harvest, the farmer decided to select one of his quails to celebrate the festivities with his family, but he could not decide which of the healthy birds would provide the most satisfaction for his table. Therefore, he sent out his son to fetch the farmer from the neighboring farm to help him decide. By the time the neighboring farmer arrived, some of the fowls were missing."

"What happened?" Raymond was regaining his composure.

"Of the family of birds, there was one who would leave the safety and comfort of the farm during feeding time to fly over the area, leaving the others huddled around the feeding bin. It was a dangerous expedition. He was confronted with dangers along the way. Carnivorous creatures and hunters ready to devour him at a moment's notice were a living reality. He did this because he understood something the others did not. He understood that the one who feeds him does so for one purpose and one purpose only. He didn't figure this out because he was necessarily smarter than the other quails or wasn't hungry for the master's food. He did this because his eyes were opened. They were opened because he left the limitations of his master's farm, traveled to all the farms, and saw other birds like him being groomed and fattened—and eventually slaughtered for their meat. The meat was no more free than the feathered fellows who watched it snatched from their midst. Raymond, what gave the fowl the idea to abandon the comfort of his farm to venture out to the other farms?"

Raymond asks, "Is it because he didn't like the farmer?"

The father responds, "No, my son. That is not it. The farmer was a master of husbandry, a good farmer who knew his purpose. The brave quail knew his purpose too and soon realized it was not inside the four squares of the farms. So, while others fed at the hands of their masters on the very thing that will destroy them, you, my son, open your eyes beyond this and free yourself. Son, pray to the Most High to reveal your purpose to you. It is then that you will be truly free. As a free man, you will have the capacity to liberate others, like the liberating quail in the riddle I have written for you. I caution you on the perils of leading a liberation. Never allow your ego to interfere with the work of the Almighty. Keep your eyes open to the things that are unseen. They will be revealed to you by the Almighty if your heart is just and you fear the Most High."

"What must I do to gain wisdom, and how will I know that my eyes are closed?" Raymond asks.

His father pauses and smiles. "This is the beginning of understanding." He opens the *Book of Wisdom and Salvation* and points to a verse. "If you want to know if your eyes are opened and that you are not in fact in a deep sleep, an illusion of some sort, read this. If you open the *Book of Wisdom and Salvation* and this passage is missing, you are asleep."

"Yes, Papa, but there is so much to learn, and so much I do not understand," Raymond replies.

His father folds his hand and looks into his son's eyes. "It begins with your mind."

Raymond asks, "What is mind, Father?"

"It is not the combination of memory and intelligence, Son. It is much more. We can only think from the facts of our reality of this world—that of which we have gathered over time. We cannot think something absolutely new. It goes against the nature of the mind. You can only recycle the past. This speaks to the notion that when you come to know that you do not know, you will begin to come close to wisdom. The Most High God, creator of mind, he who is not limited by time, the past, present, and the future, is the only one who gives wisdom. You must revere him and submit to him, and then you will find wisdom. Come, my son, and drink your mother's treatment. It's getting cold. You will need the revitalization."

In the summer, Raymond is introduced to the headmaster of the university who will carry out his father's teachings years later.

CHAPTER
TEN

...

The Speech

"Checkmate!" shouts an old man in the corner of a busy street. The other players remove their hats and slide away from the table. Up the hill, posh homes are cradled between lush trees and schoolchildren gather for shaved ice in green courtyard gardens. "Raymond, you must hurry—or we will be late for service. I am not going to miss your father's speech," an indistinctive French voice yells from the courtyard. The soft voice is covered with sounds of marketers passing by with bundles of merchandise upon their heads, dodging vintage Peugeots and trotting horses. The fighting lions shrouded in dust race past large diesel trucks carrying imported goods, maneuvering through traffic to make their deadlines.

"Raymond, hurry," exclaims the melodious voice.

Dashing downstairs, jumping over imported flowerpots near his father's library, Raymond drops the daily newspaper with the front page facing up. It reads, "New ministries Created for a Progressive Folium." He makes it to the automobile with the satisfaction of not spoiling his mother's mood. As the leather-lined import drives off, Raymond peers into the rearview mirror and waves good-bye to the footmen and maids.

Jacqueline steps into the narrow road and stoutly waves back while mouthing inaudibly to Raymond. With a puzzled face, he gazes out of his window. He looks back again and faintly sees her pointing to her palm. She returns her hands to her side in a smearing motion and faces them down as she follows the others back into the house. Perhaps she is reminding him of their previous talk of social concerns of peasants in the mountains. She would always pinch her palm and raise her hand to her mouth, portraying children he once saw playing with goat kneecaps. "We lived from hand to mouth, Master Raymond." He disliked being addressed as "Master Raymond," but such was the decorum. Sometimes, while sitting in the family garden, he would ask her about her hometown and times spent at Bidonville's remote countryside. Jacqueline opened his eyes to the world within his that he had never seen for himself. He heard his father speak of the sort—but in brevity.

Classism denoted certain experiences in a once-colonized district and ironically deprived the wealthier class the wealth of experiences that unite a people. She would speak of the visitors. They would come and plant seeds in the mountains, and they watched them grow over the years. The forests remained vast into the decades but progressively diminished as the trees were regularly uprooted for fuel. More would come and plant trees, but those did not last long either. Like the ones planted one hundred years before, others saw it as a better investment to educate the people in conservation, principles, and skills that were long forgotten or replaced by discouragement or urban migration. Time has seen this as a beneficial investment for the people of Bidonville—but not enough for a dramatic change. Jacqueline lamented on not having the opportunity for an education. She spoke of her ailing mother who lives in the countryside and brother who serves as a library courier in Roulerville.

Raymond said, "As the scholar from the East once said, 'If your plan is for one year, plant rice. If your plan is for ten years, plant trees. If your plan is for one hundred years, educate children.' That is where I believe we have failed."

Jacqueline never quite convinced Raymond why the wealthy lived in the hills, the middle class at the foot of the hills, and the poor below in small, sketchily built shacks. Her premise was that their civilization was established by inhabitants who did not go there by choice, but through exile, against their will, whether it was to fortify a growing labor force or deportation for civil violators. He was impressed by her mind. While absent a formal education, it was full of information and insight. Her confidence, despite her speech impediment, wasn't like what he expected from a peasant from the countryside. It is not that she was not arrogant or proud. She was distinguished in her own unsophisticated way.

"We started fragmented and are still till this day. The wealthiest of the population had advantages that saw them through generations," Jacqueline said.

"But what were those advantages?" Raymond asked.

"Capital, money, land, or perhaps some sort of connection to families living in Damascus, the Rhine, or someplace else." His questions remained unanswered—or at least the ones he kept in his head—because he did not want to appear unaware or foolish to an undereducated servant who knew a little more about life than many in his educated district.

Raymond buttons his vest, looks at his mother, and smiles.

Sarah smiles back, fixes his black bowtie, and brushes lint off of his back. "Someday, you will open doors for many," she tells him.

They drive past political advertisements onto a long stretching road.

Crowds make their way into the National Cathedral, shuffling between aged mahogany pews and looking for a perfect view of the pulpit.

Raymond steps out of his automobile in elegant, metal-buckled brown shoes. The speaker can be heard from the entrance hall as Raymond makes his appearance. "Peace be with you. It is with mixed emotions that I stand here before you this afternoon, commissioned by our Lord to usher his will. I have no pleasure in this task as I stand here. I, however, with dread of what tomorrow will bring, must speak to my people, to our nation, as times are dire. It would be impertinent of us to ignore them."

The speaker comes into sight, looks down to Raymond, holds on to the two corners of the stand, and smiles at his family. Pressing down on his bottom lip, he surveys the room. Raymond sits to listen to his father speak. "Martin Niemöller said it best when he amplified our quest. Except in our time, they have not come for the Socialist. They have not come for the trade unionist, our Hebraic brothers, or any other particular nation's people as in the past."

The crowd braces themselves as Reimonde speaks. He holds back tears and attempts to control his quivering lips.

"If we don't defend our countrymen now, they will soon come for us— and then there will be no one else left. It's interesting how time seems to repeat itself and how short a memory we have, but if I could take a lesson from history's classroom and share it with you today, I would begin with our past. After all, isn't it what we have as our gift to future generations, lessons from the past? If I were a man peering down from a high mountain and looking down at the immensity of human history, I would expect to see the history of man no longer in its original solid form. I would anticipate seeing a shattered mosaic of a multitude of pieces fragmented into lesser portions of itself—into morsels of time, each unable to reconnect with its former self, but reflecting, instead, a continuum of times. I would expect to see, in each time, man attempting to describe former times and future times and even the very small portion of time in which he finds himself. He is incapable of seeing them with pure clarity because these segments of time are opaque to his eye. Obscurity would have already taken its form and caused reality of the truth, the eternal, the Most High to alter with each new scheme and new ideas born under the sun.

"And if the Almighty reigning above me were to ask me to choose a time, a people, and a place to read his letters, I would ask to look beyond to the levels of his heavens. There, I would ask my Lord to send me on a mental flight. Perhaps he would send me on over to Pharaoh's Egypt, soaring above towering pyramids and other man-made galactic marks, around by the desert road, and on toward the water's mouth. I would marvel at the parting Red Sea and gaze at the faces of the six hundred thousand crossing through the desert on toward the promised land. There, I would begin to read his love letter.

"I would continue reading of His mercifulness as the annals unfold. I would observe from across expansive waters, the further gradual migration of nation-people into new times and under new laws, ushering with them new kings and new sprawling empires. I would expect to see emerging systems and classification of people and the subjugation of many of those people.

"I would expect to grieve as I read of His judgment. And while man, in his obscurity, would proceed in continuous motion toward the cyclical evolution of time, I would see his past, present, and future scattered beneath me like a glaring montage, fading as an ecliptic sky, shattered as I ascend back to the High Place. I would ask Jesus to send me here—near His Father, under His new time and under His new kingdom where I shall read His letters for evermore."

Reimonde's father closes with his hands extended over the crowd. "Peace be with you."

Outside, a loud explosion causes everyone's heads to turn to the direction of the sound.

"Peace. Peace! My brothers and sisters! Peace!" The priest comes behind Reimonde and shouts, "We have word that a curfew is in effect. All here must take precautions, go home, and care for your families."

Raymond and his mother run to the pulpit and exit into the unlit portion of the cathedral, away from the murmur and confusion. The Moyennes make it to their automobile and escape the scene.

CHAPTER
ELEVEN

...

The University

Staring down a long, partially lit hallway with an endless wall of columns and windows, Raymond waits for the approaching footsteps to come closer into view. The methodical steps become more and more apparent as the people approach. Eventually appearing as an aged man with a long white beard, he stands still. Raymond prostrates with a half bow and takes a passive stance.

The figure firmly plants his feet on the floor, takes a ready stance, and maintains a combative form. As though painting with an imaginary brush, he swipes his open hand in the air in various directions and then brings them to a close.

Raymond does not know what to make of this gesture or how to respond and takes a few steps backward. He can hear footsteps as they shuffle toward the gates. He is stunned by the deathly silent hall and looks behind him for an escape, but the large door behind him is closed. The man shouts, "Mr. Raymond!"

The young scholar is frightened and wonders what is to become of him. He tightens his fist as instructed by his father and shivers from his wild imagination and the possible outcomes. He takes in a deep breath and lightly closes his eyes. Inhale and a slow release. All of a sudden, he hears his name again surrounding him. "Mr. Raymond!"

He instantly opens his eyes, and as the brilliant light behind the man draws closer, he hears the call a third time, "Mr. Raymond!"

He replies with what his father taught him: "If it is the voice of the Lord who calls, I answer with, here am I Lord." Raymond recalls this as one of the riddles to the entrance gate.

The aged man replies, "Mr. Raymond, today is the first day of the rest of your life, in which you will become a master of your mind, for the mind is the standard of the man."

In the days to come, Raymond would undergo rigorous spiritual teachings, meditation, and the art of mental defenses. In classroom one where young boys begin the first month of training, Raymond stands attentively as the teacher silently enters the room. This time, the teacher's footsteps can't be heard as before in the entry halls.

Without acknowledging the line of students with backs straightened up and eyes fixed forward, they wait for his command. He inspects them for form and strength. "Mr. Raymond!" he sternly calls, startling another boy at the end of the line. The teacher turns his head to the center of the line, shifts direction toward Raymond, and slowly walks over to the nervous teen. He hands him a closed scroll and gestures for him to follow. Raymond bows and follows the professor to an enclosed courtyard surrounded by pebbles and gentle streams. The other boys remain in attention, listening to the training on the other side of the large doors.

A compelling battle that defies physical limitations runs the course for hours, piquing their curiosity of what Raymond is being taught or being subjected to. They hear the sliding of feet as a chess piece moves on a congested board. "You enter here, defeat the knight, and now pivot and turn to the next stronghold, remove the first column. Yes! Now strike again, change position, go. Go … go … yes! Now sack the king!" the teacher commands on the other side of the door.

At the end of the training, Raymond is instructed to open the scroll. It reads, "Finally, my brethren, be strong in the Lord, and in the power of his might. Put on the whole armor of God that ye may be able to stand against the wiles of the evil one."

The next day, Raymond returns from an exercise to sack agents of the queen of the coast. Breathing heavily and under great distress, he enters the teacher's court.

"Teacher, teacher, I have returned from the village." Still breathing heavily as his chest rise and lowers, he tries to complete his sentences. "I tried to tear down the stronghold, but it was not working the way I thought it would. The way you taught me. It was not working the way you told me. I tried. I repeated the passages from the three bridges, the one of the Mediator, the Light, and the Father. I called it out with conviction, but the agents would not come out. I fought them all throughout the magical hours to no avail."

The teacher replies in a husky voice, "Son, let me tell you one important thing you have neglected to remember. You cannot come before a man and carry him out of his prison, snatch him from between the bars of his mind, and expect him to love you for his freedom. He does not know that he is bound and loves his condition. He will hate you for it. No! You must lure him out from his bondage by defeating what bounds him. Lazarus was never taken out of his tomb! He was called out of his tomb! Don't you ever go into the enemy's camp unaware of this truth! Your enemy is very, very cunning."

"Yes, teacher," Raymond replies with his head bowed.

The teacher, with both arms folded behind his back and hands tucked into his sleeves, comes closer to Raymond. "Come with me on a journey into a city that will defy the illusions you have accepted as reality, where you will better understand the totality of the lessons in classroom one and never again question your ability to break a stronghold of any village."

They enter the gates of a majestic city.

Overwhelmed by the limitlessness of the place, Raymond lightly closes his eyes and calls, "Teacher?" He still sees whatever he saw before. Astonished by this marvel, he calls again, "Teacher, what is this place?"

"Patience, son. You shall soon see," he replies.

They walk past marvelous streams of light, shooting out of an array of moving spheres. On the backs of giant mountains, they ascend to majestic towers surrounded by streams of more light and then between a market square. The teacher looks to Raymond and says, "Are you ready?

Raymond replies, "Yes."

The teacher replies, "Raymond, what you are observing is a small region of a great city. One is a mirror of a physical reality you must understand to hold dominion. It is your mind, Raymond. It is the reality you have created."

Raymond quickly replies, "Whoa. My apologies, Teacher, and excuse me for my disbelief, but I don't understand."

The teacher points to towers and a massive cathedral. "Look there. What do you see?"

Raymond hears the tolling of a large bell and turns to the teacher. "I see a tower."

He replies, "No. Look again, Raymond. What do you see?"

Raymond inhales, releases slowly, and relaxes his nerves.

"Yes. Change your perspective and see beyond what is there." The teacher grins as he observes Raymond's reaction to the revelation. "Yes, son. Now, what do you see?"

Raymond swells up with emotions.

"Yes, Raymond. You built this—all of this, the mountains, the streams, and the monumental towers. They represent the creations of your mind. When you meditate on love, you begin to build a tower of its likeness. When you meditate on justice, you lay down the foundations to another tower. When you meditate on the Most High, you position the center of the city around the cathedral."

The bell tolls a second time.

"In the short period you have lived, you have built a metropolis of the things you allow to enter your mind."

Suddenly, a giant whale ejects from the waters into the air and punctures the surface of the water, submerging to the depths of the blue sea.

"There will be those who will try to raid and subjugate your city, your towers, and even your cathedral. Their intention is to force you to build an alternative city, their city, and then once under siege, imprison you there as their slave. In this desolate city, they will harvest more minds into a different kind of tower that will reach the heights of the heavens—and they will sit on the throne. Are you ready for submission to the Most High, God? Are you willing to learn the nature of the mind, your thoughts, and how to defend the gates of your mind, Mr. Raymond?"

Raymond bows and says, "Yes. Yes. Teach me, Master."

"The cathedral is your sanctum pine. Enter and see if the beauty of his holiness is on the throne. See if the Most High sits on the throne and reigns and if the center of your mind, the essence of your soul, submits to our Lord."

As they enter the cathedral, the massive whale emerges from the sea and emits a low frequency, which increases to a sonic horn.

Raymond is suddenly awakened in his bed by the sound of a ram's horn. "Whoa, what a dream!" he says with relief. He jumps from his disheveled bed, stands, and observes writings on the wall. "Oh my soul! The time has come, and I have awakened from my sleep."

Raymond imprints the warm floor as he makes his way to a small table fitted with unleavened bread and herbal tea. Beside it, a golden bell draws his curiosity to the meaning of the display. Before sampling a morsel, he bows his head, and with his hands stretched out, he prays to the Most High. Between each prayer, he turns in the direction of north, east, south, and west, declaring the promises written in the *Book of Wisdom and Salvation* and establishing spiritual authority in each point. "Thank you, Jesus," he whispers as he takes his first bite.

Ma Jolie

Years later, Raymond has grown into a mature young man. Escaping the heat of the summer, Raymond and his friends join many other students seeking leisure at Plage D'ore Bleau. He wades in the water into the better part of the shoreline, soaking in the sunshine and sparkling blue waters of the private beach.

He notices a group of young ladies not too far from where he and his comrades set up camp. A local guitarist entertains them as they enjoy morsels of spicy conch served in coconut shells. Swimming against the tides, he approaches their position for a closer look and recognizes one of the ladies as his beloved Jolie. Eventually, the girls decide to go into the water, but Jolie stays behind.

Sitting alone, perhaps in deep thought, she stares into the horizon. The blue Atlantis wind embraces the curves of her modesty, never revealing the forbidden—only the evidence of God's gifted hands. It blows through her smooth, black, silky hair, tasking her with the chore of uncovering her beautiful face, revealing long lashes that could cast a thousand nets into the sea if she had to. The innocence in her brown eyes draws Raymond's heart closer to a possibility that seems so far. Her symmetrically proportionate display of beauty and wonder warms the blood in his veins and throbs his heart with vigor and more life, the type that emboldens a man to fight wars in the name of a woman's honor or to lay down his life to protect her virtue.

Wisdom and virtue highlight her face, and modesty adorns her like a princess disguised as a maiden waiting for her prince. A mélange of tamed beauty and quality tugs at Raymond's heart.

Sitting quietly and admiring the expression of the ocean, she closes her eyes and smiles as if to a love story in her mind that only she can hear. Inhaling the light mist of the white foaming waves, she takes in light and gentle breaths. Raymond, on the other hand, breathes heavily, wishing himself as the narrator and principal character in her fantastic love story in which he woos her with laughter.

Beyond the large boulders encasing the busy beach, an isolated horse stable is nestled between several mature coconut palms. At the entrance, a female tourist with local flowers tucked in her hair poses for a scenic picture. Holding a cluster of tropical flowers in her hand, she smiles at a man wearing an equestrian helmet. This image gives Raymond a short-ranged idea. He decides to run back to his camp to fulfill his brilliant plan.

His friends are occupied with a competitive game of soccer. "Hey, Raymond, where are you going?"

He hurriedly replies, "To get a better view." As a gallant victor of war emerging from the sand dune spirals of Freeland, he surfaces on horseback, galloping to where he expects to find Jolie, but she is longer there. Raymond moves about in every direction. Like a champion polo player pursuing his prize, he searches for the evasive Ma Jolie with zeal. Laboriously climbing the stone embankment with hopes that she has not ventured far from the beach, he reins the horse for the pursuit. "Ya. Ya. Ya!" he shouts, but as time passes, he soon realizes that her presence has evaded him.

Later that night, under the reflection of a bright moon, he laments the lost opportunity. The embarrassingly uneventful attempt to contact Jolie is met with discouragement. He envisions the day when he rides with her into the sunset or holds her hand in the mountain forest. Her sparkling brown eyes would look into his as her caramel skin rubs against him. His mind labors day and night with these thoughts as one infected by a malady of love. While pacing in his room, he talks to himself and imagines the conversations he would have, which has never left his lips. In his mind, this queen of Bidonville has earned a rightful position as queen of his heart. He is her king. When reality visits and reminds him that he is a mere pauper in the territory of love, he bows his head in distress.

Wrestling with this actuality, he tries to suppress her in his thoughts, but she reappears in a captivating fragrance that intensifies with each passing breeze. Over and over again, love wins the battle over logic and reason, filling him with unfulfilled desire. In his eyes, there is no other. He is faced with a dichotomy that is ever present in their culture. He is a Moyenne, and she is forever a Jolie.

Greater than his most exaggerated imagination, he finds himself foolishly and maddeningly in love, dangerously gripping a notion that is as concrete as vapor in the wind. To lessen its pains, he decides to write Jolie a letter. As he begins to formulate words he considers as appropriate for an unconfirmed relationship, his mother calls him downstairs.

Raymond answers, "Yes, Mother. I will be there in a moment." He writes the first few words of his love letter before heading downstairs: Ma Jolie, the sunshine of my day, tonight I decided to write what my heart could best say on paper that my lips could never utter in words."

The pen is soon stifled by another call. "Raymond! Your father wants you to meet him in the vineyard."

Raymond runs down to the great room, and his mother leans toward rolls of fabric. "Before you go, my son, you are going to have to tell me what is on your mind. I have sensed all day that something is weighing heavily on your heart." She invites him to sit beside her. "You must have found love. Are you in love, Raymond?"

Raymond answers, "Mother, you know me so well. Yes, my heart has been captured by the professor's daughter, but I am barred by barriers I cannot control."

"My son, love is not like the wind to be cast in the direction you cannot see, the projector of your heart's desire, or wherever the paths of your heart lead you. Love has its principles. Tell me what her father thinks of you?"

"I do not reach his high standard, Mother, but this is not a foolish love," replies Raymond.

"I tell you this? Are you listening?" his mother asks.

"Yes, Mother. I am."

"Raymond, you must not cross over the sacred boundaries. Instead, respect them. You must search for the love of her mother and the respect of her father. Once you reach that destination, you will find the one you so love."

A couple of months into the season, on the busy roads to the hills of Bidonville, Raymond stops to smell a bouquet of violets and red roses. He approaches one of the merchants and asks for the freshest cut for a lady worthy of the best. The two sisters who manage the small roadside boutique compliment Raymond for his taste but caution him on the perils of love. He smiles, but their words are drowned out by Ma Jolie's melodic voice in his ears. The way she pronounces his name in an accent unique to the high-class girls from the hills tickles his ears. Before she ever knew his name, playfully enunciated the letters of his name, or noticed that he existed, he remarked on the beauty of her ways. He watched and observed from afar how she speaks to her father, her obedience to her mother even when scorned for neglecting her minor household tasks, and the compassion she has for her older sisters. He respected her from afar and directed admiration to her in his heart. Day after day, he scrutinized her without building up the confidence to share his inner heart. With a bouquet of flowers, Raymond arrives at the impressive neighborhood lined with gated homes and fanning palm trees.

He chimes the golden bell and waits for a response. From the small glass in the door, he sees the rhythmic silhouette approaching. To his delight, he is greeted by a gentle display of beauty and grace. "Oh Raymond, how are you, *mon frere*? How nice to see you on this chilly afternoon. What cool breeze brings you here at this hour?"

"I came by to see you, Jolie," he nervously replies after removing an anxious hand from his pocket and placing it behind his back. "Would you be interested in going for a walk in the center garden?"

"Let me ask my father," she replies.

Her father is a pretentious man, quite particular in his tastes and firm on his principles. As a well-read attorney of Bidonville, he argues the social injustice of the people of Folium on paper, but rarely in practice. The professor is more of a thinker than an executioner of ideas. Sitting in his well-lit library in his favorite leather chair, he reads a book on the prejudices of the heart. His purebred at his feet and a small cup of dark roast on his coffee table, he loses himself in the literature. He has a taste for the finer things in life and wants the same for his family, including the caliber of men. "Who are you talking to, dear?"

"It's Raymond, Papa." She knows the likelihood is slim that she will be permitted to go with Raymond. "He has invited me to an evening walk at the center garden. May I go, Papa?"

Raymond also knows the custom is that young ladies are not to be seen with the opposite gender in public without an accountable witness. Frequently, her older sisters would accompany her for these walks and assumes this would be the arrangement again. He hoped they would come along and follow several feet behind as they visit the local creamier together. A casual walk to the center garden was not an act of commitment and should be seen as friendly gesture. He optimistically hoped that would be the case tonight, despite the short notice.

Looking down at the base of his reading glasses, he says "*D 'Ore*! Tell him no. You have studies to attend to and cannot join him for walks. I don't want my daughters spending their time wandering around with a *Rien à Faire*. Why don't you find something to do that is more worthy of your day?"

"But, Papa he is just a kind friend," Jolie whispers.

Raymond rubs his chest as though stricken with a sudden bout of indigestion. When she returns to the door, he assures her that they could walk some other time and that he respects her father's wishes. He bids her a good evening.

Walking home that night, he questioned if the professor's rejection was out of principle or because he was a Moyenne, a child of an African Hebrew, living in a fictitious world.

He returns to the peaceful, bare streets of the hills. Canals deliver petals of violets and red roses from the hills, along with small debris and rubbish that the shanties are always left with to dispose of. He sees life's satire at play. What goes up must eventually come down. His raging emotion slowly calms with the hopes of speaking when his approach is appropriately performed. He counts his footsteps and imagines them next to Ma Jolie—each step a musical note with fate as the conductor.

Years later, as an esteemed enrollee of the University of Roulerville, Raymond is mastering the art of mathematics and philosophy as taught to him by Folium's system. It was not until he traveled beyond the outlying districts that his perspective of the world changed. As a transient apprentice of the eastern districts of Freeland, Raymond begins to question his formal education. Throughout his travels and collaboration, he was able to unearth suppressed truths of his heritage and others like him in Folium. There were many refugees and stateless men and women who crossed his path. From their experiences, he learned much of himself. He grew to value himself more and have a meaningful love for God.

Regarding international social studies, he discovered that universally, the refugee is metaphorically bonded to the borders of his constitution. Repeating the bearings of his forefather, he toils in motionless progress to his inevitable supinus state. He dreams of better days and formulates a scheme to improve his condition in spite of past failures, but like his forefather, he relents to the bitter reality that surrounds him. He is merely a pebble in the world's shoe.

Besieged by tenuous governance, he embraces what is familiar and learns to pacify the impending conundrum that is heading toward him. As a citizen of this life, he learns to dip his hardened bread in a borrowed cup, which his ancestors once help form and fill.

History has already given him a glimpse into his future. It was written in his native tongue and scribed in the world's edition of *meritless*. Its first chapter, written in crimson, was embroiled into the fabric of his flag and strife-filled existence. Outside the borders of his district, his name denoted a pariah fleeing from a devalued land with nothing of value to offer the rest of the world. Others who fell victim to this prejudgment abandoned their nation for where the promise of security, sustenance, and self-development is assured. Whether by rafts or through the porous borders of greater districts, he runs toward the land of the free and the brave. Wisdom, however, whispers in his ear, and if he understood her, she would teach him this fact that when a man begins to think less of himself or his homestead as unworthy, he has already devalued his worth to the world, his home, and the fruits of his labor will be for naught. Although his anthem is incredulous before his current circumstance, he subscribes to it and identifies with it and vows to make his land glorious again.

On a gracious afternoon, Raymond attends an opera, which tells a story of a man who loses three silver coins. The largest one had an impression of a lady heralding liberty. The other two of smaller value remained beside her on each side. They are unnoticed on the busy streets of the financial district. Another man, the Operaist, is singing. He comes close, waits for the cars to pass, and tries to retrieve the coins, but they are in front of a gate protected by armed guards. He steps away only to watch several soldiers from the First or perhaps the Second World War arrive to see her. The rare coin glistens in the sun, and they drag the larger coin away. Suddenly, they dive into the coin, entering into her time in history and taking advantage of her vulnerability. The man desiring the lost coins abandons the district and runs away in horror.

Raymond is impressed by the allegory and takes notice of the well-dressed socialites and commoners in attendance and thinks that music is indeed the universal language that unites us to a common idea. How splendid a medium to communicate ideas overlooked by the masses. As the percussions increase, he resumes his thoughts on the state of the refugee. As the homeless chooses his home without consideration, so does the bohemian who, in his domicile, is as volatile as his condition. A man without a nation to speak of finds himself in the same predicament. Perhaps it is of caution that Folium speaks not of this great tragedy of modern society, but a ringing question remains: What is to become of a man whose nomadic quest comes to the point of mere survival? I will go to wherever there is bread. Perhaps tomorrow will unfold a new chapter for exiles of Bidonville—not written about stateless men and women but respected members of the human race. The subtitle would no longer read, "A searcher of a 'trenche-de-vie,' but a victor and an equal contributor to the world's advancement. Raymond joins the assembly in a standing ovation as tears stream down his cheeks.

As a student of the philosophy of life, Raymond seeks to quench his thirst for knowledge and information by paying a visit to the university library. He runs into his overachieving classmates, Alexandria and Professor Gujarat's daughter, Siddis.

"Raymond, don't forget the study group is meeting today to discuss the chapters on the rise and fall of Egyptian dynasties. Siddis's great grandparents voyaged from Kush to the westernmost part of Bharat, one of the eastern districts, and established one of the largest import empires in their sub-district, raising the family from the ranks of petite bourgeois to one of the great bourgeoisie in the district. Her great-grandfather, one of Bharat's top admirals, once traveled to Freeland and led a spiritual revolution in the region, but he underestimated the hazard. Ultimately, religious persecution forced them into exile.

Years later, the successful importing enterprise suffered under the effects of opportunism and the exploits of interconnected trade alliances. The Gujarats have not returned since.

"Siddis and I are planning to lead the discussion," says Alexandria.

They are both majoring in archeology and genealogy. They look forward to the study groups and encourage commitment from their cohorts. In conversations, Alexandria shared how she overcame the disdain imposed upon her because of her dark skin by learning of her genealogy. Raymond was able to relate to both women in that regard, but his admiration for Alexandria was limited by her yielding to pride and historical prejudices. There is much to be refrained from in that sort of thinking because her abstinence from opposing cultures will lead her to buy further into the Folium's deception. This substitute for practicality is what has kept the continent so well divided, leading its districts into a dead end. Through her academic development, he hoped she would come to a new perspective.

Raymond replies, "Bien sûr," and walks toward the quarterly reviews section. He comes across a publication featuring an article on declassified information recently released by the ministry of truth. He finds discomfort in their manipulation of what is sold to the people as the truth. In his reading, he tries to relive the emotions shared by his mother when she dramatized the moment spent crouched in a small room, hoping not to be noticed by the raiders. She compared her experiences to that of the characters in Plato's telling of the cave. As a clear thinker, Raymond associated her accountings with his father's political frame of reference.

It was as though the mélange of life events surrounding them in the country they loved was seen from their unique perspective: the perspective of the privileged. They needed to experience a raid themselves to fully appreciate the gravity of the district's condition. It was not that they did not give to the poor or live righteous lives. It was that reality stood still for them, flickering its impression on the confines of their life experiences. Like a cave, they were prisoners in a free world. While they knew enough not to patronize the devices that lie to their vision, they overlooked one vital fact of a free society: a legitimate democracy demands an educated and informed people. It is then they can trust their own government.

After reading through the publication, he decides to put pen to paper to reflect his thoughts but diverts for a moment to write home. He opens by reminding his father and mother that he loves them and finds solace in that they raised him to become a young man who fears and loves God, which has proven to be an anchor in this developing life. He goes further to tell them that he will be arriving in Bidonville in the spring and anticipates seeing them and his siblings. He indulges in the memory of walks in the garden with a young girl he affectionately called "Ma Jolie Fleur." He yearned to see her again and share his newfound revelations while studying abroad.

That evening, he retired to the large rocks at the shores to reflect on his gripping emotions. Casting pebbles at the foaming waves, he positions himself to inhale the salty mists of the sea. He can hear Jolie's laughter as he articulated entertaining stories and pointed out interesting details. He recalls the night before he departed to another expedition via the district found among the autonomy-seeking Croats and west to the home of Lascaux cave. While there, he found it even harder to be away from her.

Raymond realizes his daydreaming robbed him of precious time and resumes writing. At the end of his letter to his parents, Raymond wrestles with his heart and tries to ignore her captivating fragrance that intensified his raging emotion. He calms his fire with the hopes of speaking to her again. Who else could embrace his heart like her? He ends his letter: "I pray to see you soon—just in time for the harvest."

Homecoming

In the spring, Raymond arrives in Bidonville ports and orders a taxi to take him home—in the private estates at the foot of the hills. In the following months, he was to present an address to wealthy donors of the university and felt it was best to incorporate some values in advising prudent giving and began reading passages in the *Book of Wisdom and Salvation*.

The following evening, as the piano keys pitch to the high notes and the violin strikes its final string, Raymond stands before a podium. "In the name of the merciful and magnificent God, I greet you. May his peace be with you! To the distinguished constituents, colleagues, and guests, I say to you good evening. My name is Raymond Moyenne, son of a noble immigrant from the faraway regions of Freeland. It is my pleasure to stand before you tonight to share with you principles I have learned, not from the university necessarily, but from lessons of life. As a journalist of life's events, those I am fortunate enough to have seen and hear, I deliver to you certain developments with humility, but with dexterity so as to whet your appetite for intelligent discussion.

"In my travels throughout Folium, I have come to learn more about our home here in Bidonville than ever before. My learning did not stop there. No. I learned even more of my original home in Freeland, in that place in the *Mosaic*. My father always reminded me that it's from the vines you can know the tree which bears its fruit. Those vines have come to bear and have shown me the reasons for many of our troubles all throughout Folium. From the shanties to the chalets, we suffer from the same predicament under the dominion of this kingdom. You know the hierarchy, the rulers, the authorities, and the powers of this dark world and the spiritual forces of evil in the heavenly realms. I need not delve into the details of this system and its effects, but I will point out an element not often discussed, and this is time.

"I believe you will agree with me that time is like a currency in some ways. While it is not a respecter of persons, it has its principles that yield to universal laws. The control governs the things above and the things below. Unlike currency, however, if we plunder this precious nonrenewable resource, we cannot regain it. It's gone, lost forever. This present moment in time is all we have, and we must not waste it with meaningless things. I begin by asking you this: How will you proportion it? How will you invest it? How will you spend it?"

Raymond surveys the room of elaborate gowns, Windsors, and bowties and pauses for a brief reflection. The character and atmosphere of the hall have primed it for sophisticated discourse and dialogue. Its guests, captivated by his thought-provoking remarks, invite the stillness of the air to slow down with time. The tables are quiet and attentive. They can hear their breathing where before it was the sound of wine filling up wine glasses, light chatter, and the handling of fancy plates and silverware.

"Is Bidonville running out of time—or, shall I ask, is time running from Bidonville? It depends on how one chooses to look at it, I suppose."

A servant places a half full glass of wine at the podium. Raymond looks down at the glass, sees his reflection, and allows a creative thought to enter his mind.

"Are we not mere subjects living out our lives on an artificial establishment created for us in a land we call home? For every sector, there is a rank and file, and of course, those groomed in the fifth column. For every sector, there is the misfortune of the many serving the good fortune of the few. Why must this be? I quote the philosopher from the eastern district: 'In a country, well-governed poverty is something to be ashamed of. In a country badly governed, wealth is something to be ashamed of.'

"Our district, in terms of engineering, is no different than any other throughout Folium. We live in a time-lapsed land where old ideas live and die with restraints created by our own vices. I understand that some here tonight might find what I am about to say rather reclusive, but I believe it is important that it is said for the benefit of forming a frame around an important idea. My fellow brothers and sisters here tonight, I submit to you an idea that I hope you will take to heart. It's not a new idea. No, it is as old as time. It is evicted with each generation to make room for what we conceive as new ideas, but it remains alive nonetheless." Raymond raises his wine glass and looks through its sparkle as the room's light pierces through the dark hue of the imported blend. He decides not to take a sip and replaces the clustering drink on the podium.

"We are at a precipice of change. The view of tomorrow seemed quite bleak before, but we can see it clearer now. Ascension of time along with the knowledge of man is speeding up, but to what end? The end of an age? What are our contributions to this? Some would argue there are none because, in their minds, we are not the conduit between the generations. They buy into the lie that one has nothing to do with the other. They believe falsely that they are just passing through while graduating to the levels of their own understanding.

"The limitation of our minds remains barricaded by the establishments we adopt. And what are these establishments? Look beyond the meaningless things you have come to love and look at the signs given to you by the Almighty. It's all around us. Look beyond the established order created by the lords of lands, reapers of human capital, and cultivators of souls and come to know the divine order of things.

"We are living in a quiet state of chaos, moving at a rate of a thousand miles per hour, a missile in the cosmos racing toward time, but we study the art of war and eat the bread from its gains. To what end? The Folium establishment is found in many things, but your mind above all—your only sacred sanctum pine—is where its pillars securely plant. Like the four pillars of Folium, it squarely sits in the middle of your mind. That is why we believe that it is of your will and your mind that she keeps her grip. If you build up enough spiritual fortitude and take it back, she will have nothing more than an idea. That is why the university develops programs geared to teaching the art of protecting the mind. This is where absolute freedom lives and communion with the Most High lives. The heart, the mind, the soul of humanity has eternity written in it, and its creator and the scribe are very evident.

"The establishment is at war with the collective mind, and the spoils thus far seem to be your eternity. I submit to you tonight that you engage the absolute truth and decide for yourself who will be your master. How will you spend the currency of time? Will you render unto the kings of Folium what belongs to Folium and give unto the Most High of this multiverse what belongs to the Most High? You decide. You choose whether you are free men and women or actors in a grand masquerade where bliss and indifference dictate your days.

"So, tonight, as you raise funds for the university with one hand, I urge you to consider who controls the other. Shall you finance the harvest or fund the functions that lead to the liberation of the future generations of Bidonville. I leave you with these decisions to ponder, and once again, I thank you."

As Raymond returns to his seat, the professor immediately stands up and invites Raymond to his table. Profoundly moved by Raymond's presentation, he puts all reservations aside and insists that he joins them, directing him to a chair across from Jolie. Captivated by the passion and intellectual honesty in his delivery, he wishes to discuss the topic with Raymond on a personal level.

Unlike before, Raymond is seen in a new light, not tinted by his heritage but by his character and intellect. Earning the privilege to sit at the same table with the woman he loves animates Raymond to a nervous wreck. Even his words begin to lose rhythm as he tries to apply the same flair in his speech to their light conversation. Raymond fails in that attempt. Incapable of correcting his bumbling words and hand motions, he resorts to grasping his legs to restore his nerves. This becomes apparent to Ma Jolie, and she asks her father to pour Raymond a glass of cold water.

Get yourself together, Raymond. You are making a complete fool of yourself. He fears that what initially piqued the professor's curiosity might spoil into a regretful moment for both Raymond and the professor.

"So, tell me, what your father does for a living?" asks the professor.

"Yes, sir." It is not an open-ended question, but Raymond responds as though he is preoccupied.

The professor tilts his head to suggest that he is waiting for Raymond to answer his questions. "Raymond … your father?"

"Oh, yes, Professor. Sorry. He is primarily an engineer, but he serves as an elder at the Iconium. He has written many books on various topics."

"I understand that your mother is a fashion designer, a native of … what was that district's name again?" The professor waits for Raymond to fill in the blank, but Raymond does not. "What was the name of that district again?"

Raymond begins to feel the awkwardness of the conversation and begins to utter a few words.

The fundraising director quickly interrupts him. "Excuse me, gentlemen and young lady." The director bows and greets Jolie. "Mr. Moyenne, may I ask you to join us for a photogram, pardon, I mean photograph.

"Sir, I am no illusionist," replies Raymond.

"Not at all, sir. A slip of the tongue."

"Freudian?" Raymond asks.

The director chuckles.

Saved in a nick of time, Raymond gladly excuses himself and asks the professor for another opportunity to resume their conversation.

"Ah … yes, definitely son. Would you like to join me as a guest at the gallery? There is an unveiling of imported paintings that I trust you will enjoy. There is a beautiful display of mosaic art imported from the Byzantine and Ottoman district. Here, take my card so that we may keep in touch."

Raymond replies, "I would be honored, Professor." Raymond bids Jolie and the professor a good evening.

Talks from The Heart

The following week, Raymond strolls the secluded gardens of the hills and sits on one of the unoccupied benches. Moments later, Jolie and her sisters walk by. Startled by the coincidence, she smiles, places her hands on her chest, and turns to look at her sisters. One of them whispers in her ear, and they walk away, leaving Jolie with Raymond.

Fanning her face from warm flush on her skin, she says, "Raymond, what sweet-smelling breeze brings us here this morning?"

He replies, "Your sisters have arranged for me to speak to you at the lake. Would you like to join me?"

She folds her hands in front of her and walks along the blooming flower path with Raymond. "I am leaving tomorrow and wanted to share a few words with you."

"Jolie? Jolie Fleur, may I speak to you?" beckons Raymond.

"Yes, of course, Raymond," she replies softly.

Raymond can see a restrained love in her eyes and struggles with the temptation to ask her for a commitment of her love. "Have you ever reflected on the meaning of life, where we have come from, and where we are headed?"

Her nostrils expand, and her eyes sparkle. "I have not given it much thought. What are you saying, Raymond? Is something wrong?"

He replies, "No. I am fine, Jolie. I sometimes feel as though we are living in a well-ordered, well-organized medium created by some other force to control our destiny. I don't like the idea of not controlling my own destiny." Raymond looks into her eyes. "You see, at the university, I have learned that we should not set peace as our highest goal in life. It should be a fundamental part of life. To be peaceful is the first thing in life."

"And are you at peace?" Jolie asks

"Yes, peace in knowing God is in control and that I have a relationship with him through his son Yeshua HaMashiach, Jesus the Christ. I do, however, have concerns."

"So why this sudden thought, Raymond? What distresses you?"

Casting pebbles into the lake, he replies, "See these ripples?"

"Yes. I do," she replies while tightly pressing on the blossomed petals in her hands.

"They are like the pattern of our lives."

Jolie laughs and pats him on the shoulder, "Raymond, come on. Are you going to speak philosophy to me again on such a lovely day by the lake?"

Raymond laughs. "Jolie, allow me to share my thoughts with you this one more time." He observes the pearly white of her smile, perfection in her skin, the sparkle in her brown eyes and says, "Jolie?"

She replies, "Yes. I am listening."

Raymond snaps out from the momentary allure of her beauty and resumes his original thought.

"So, if life is spent in the pursuit of peace, then we would have wasted parts of it and failed at the first test in life. If this is so, the way we feel about ourselves right now determines the quality of our lives—and not the things around us. Does peace exist in our minds? If it does, what are we allowing to dominate our minds? If in my mind, for example, I were to look into the center of my soul, would I find peace? If my mind were a city where towers of worry and failures littered its corners, what type of city would it be? Would I want to live there—or would I recognize them for what they are and tear down the strongholds and build towers of greatness and godliness instead? Would I build a city of love, a city where two lovers would no longer be afraid to sing I love you?"

Raymond and Jolie's eyes lock, and they draw closer to each other. She slowly lowers her head to avoid a kiss.

Raymond holds her chin, smiles, and whispers in her ear, "Ma Jolie, you are virtuous woman, true and true. For this, I tell you I love you."

CHAPTER
TWELVE

•••

Control Out of Order

A large man in a dark suit walks in and sits at the center of a cigar smoke-filled room. Several other men accompany him. His shiny black shoes plant firmly on the bright, reflective floor as he surveys the room. "Gentlemen, as you were," he says.

The floor resembles a large chessboard and reproduces the large crystal and gold chandelier hovering above as in the symmetric painting fixed to the wall.

"I was never much of a sympatric man even in the slightest form of the word, but I have come to realize that we change, or more precisely, time changes us. For some us here, we become something else." The thick-lipped man points to a map of Bidonville. He removes the partially smoked cigar and taps it into an ashtray. He releases several rings of smoke in the direction of the shadowy figures as they patiently wait for the man to continue.

"Gentlemen of Exiled Kings, revolution, and evolution from the masses are inevitable. Is it for naught that we tighten our grip and hasten the agenda?"

The room illuminates with the slow draw of metallic curtains, revealing cascading sunlight through the dusty windows, reflecting the hour of the day. From the left corner of the hazy room, a tall, slender man comes into focus with a dense envelope in his hand. He walks over to the head of the table and gives the package to the thick-lipped man.

In a baritone voice, the man says, "What we must do here is not for our sake, gentlemen, but in the interests of Folium and the family. We have our orders, gentlemen. If we fail, it will cost us dearly. We will have to answer to the Olympians and their courts." He opens the envelope and reads it contents.

Aghast, the thick-lipped man looks up with a stern gaze, passes the paper to the next man, sits down, and turns his back on the beveled edge of the table. Facing the exposed window, he says, "We mustn't ever allow them to change masters before the eve of the harvest—or we will find something that will be greater than any plan we can deliver. They must be kept distracted by the trivial things at all costs if we are to succeed."

The peculiar papers in the envelope had several agenda items. One of which is the proposition to the citizenry that taxes would be levied on the wealthy of society to fund social programs and a larger national protection force to secure Folium's interests and borders. This would be the simple and less invasive, created to support the financial district. The other items require the redefinition of all things sacred and the fluidity of spirituality of Folium and reverence to the name of the Most High. The third item is the systematic integration of humans into the microchip system. Access to Folium would be granted and terminated at the push of a button.

The unrevealed scheme would have exposed itself years later when the popular ploy would be imposed on the rest of the Folium, but it would be too late by then. The more critical items would be organized outside of Continuum by the cosmic families. The challenge in executing such a diabolical plan is the wrestling and arching the will of the people and preventing an impetus for another revolution.

One of the earlier plans to take claim over the essence of every child born under the royal seal had been successful for centuries and served as a blueprint for the series of changes to come.

War would be more frequent and of longer duration, and in every Folio cycle, the people will be pledged as collateral to the cosmic families before every harvest. Well into their age of production, for those who survive, the fruits of their labor will create a consistent agreement to further entangle them in a life of contractual debt. What lies ahead, hidden in the agenda, is the fate of Folium: liberation or damnation of its people.

CHAPTER
THIRTEEN

•••

Valley of Decision

The heat of the market square hovers over the brows of brightly dressed pedestrians tunneling through the busy morning crowd and searching for bargains. Many gather in narrow sidewalks, in front of wooden charcoal wagons, and some fish in short barrels for tropical fruit. Every vendor station is filled with an assortment of local goods. The morning mist, barely evaporated on the tin rooftops, shines brightly on carefully dangling plants perched on balconies. It soon disappears to the brightening sun.

Trucks and private vehicles entering the market honk their horns at inattentive ears moving in various directions. Businessmen, school children, housewives, and servants fill the crossroads, creating more congestion.

The air is filled with a mixed bowl of spicy grilled peanuts, roasted coffee beans, and fluffy baked bread. In another block, grilled meats bathe in steamy pots and compete with creameries and freshly squeezed orange and papaya blends. This is the nature of the markets, capturing the essence of the countryside and reintroduced at the square.

In the docility of the air, a small leaf begins to spin in the whirlwind from the apex of two busy roads near the market square. The bright green specimen moves toward the thirteenth streets of Bidonville where it is captured by the wind's ascent, floating high above the tall tropical trees hugging the streets of Rome, Corinth, and Galatia. Like a feather from a high-flying bird, it is plucked down and chased by the wind's purposeful direction. Its broad blades cooperate with its undertaking in an acrobatic spin and flip as it steadily climbs toward the sun. Moments later, it descends in the shadows of archaic buildings of the capital, coming to a stop at the crossroads. In a sudden gust, it is again lifted and captured by the swiftness of foot traffic finding its way to the market square, and there, it finds rest among the crowd. It remains halted there throughout the time-consuming hour.

Behind one of the fruit barrels, a well-dressed man accepts an offer for a shoeshine.

The shoeshine boy soon discovers that he has a problem as he reluctantly wipes away the dust from the shoes. He only has black and two shades of brown available in his wooden box—not the distinct earth-leather hue the well-dressed man is wearing. "Mister, I didn't realize that your shoes didn't match my browns."

The man smiles, places the money into the boy's box, and walks toward the gathering crowd. Streaks of yellow ribbons dress up the tents, and exposed aluminum sheets reflect the morning sky.

He walks past Marche Noir, toward other merchants holding baskets above their heads. Some sell thinly threaded towels, imported water, and others peddle makeshift toys with parts obviously repurposed from rejected trinkets and doodads.

He makes his way in the circle and finds another young man with a hat and a worn-out black and brown bag. He occasionally waves the *Book of Wisdom and Salvation* in the air as he composes his impactful delivery.

The well-dressed man removes a letter from his coat pocket. "Dear Mr. Raymond, our collaborative efforts have received great responses from our Magma brothers in the south district. We anticipate your acquaintance in the mission and the fruits it will bear in your contact with Dan, a young convert, who has successfully championed a local revolution, bringing souls to the kingdom. We trust it will be quite eventful. This is your first mission upon arriving at the square. You will recognize his distinct Arabic accent when you meet him, but you must challenge him with the sacred parts from the passage to authenticate his identity. One of our covert agents will be present at the square to guide you if you are unable to locate him. You must not task yourself with searching for the agent, for he will find you."

The lonely leaf finds company among other leaves, after traveling in the direction of the light wind, but it soon departs, captured again by another gust of wind, finagling throughout the stages of the wind and finally rests beside the gates in front of the town, at the entrance of the portals. Sunlight shines through its small, netted veins, evaporating small spotted dewdrops.

Raymond stops to pay attention to the unusual placement of a single leaf in the middle of the town entrance and bends down to place it in his coat pocket.

Raymond and Dan Meet

Looking up, he believes he has identified Dan and prepares to address him as a gentleman, but he hesitates on the setting and environment. Dan confidently stands on a crate among a crowd, awaiting bevies of onlookers. He appears less sophisticated and rather saturated by his presentation. Dan exclaims, "My dear brother and sisters, there is nothing new under the sun."

These few words compel memories of a familiar speech given by his father, Reimonde, many years ago to a congregation who were entering a revolutionary period of Folium. In Raymond's adulthood, Folium is now doing the same, unraveling into yet another silent but impactful revolution.

"How quickly we forget this truth and readily repeat its wager time and time again, time after time. Wake up, you sleeping sluggards, slaves to the self and the here and now. Awake from this farm you have found yourself in to see Folium's true condition. You soon forget yesterday and quickly accept the bondages of today as new, altogether repackaged as chains of new schemes. I tell you that there is no other peace but the one found in the Most High. Through his mediator, we come to know his will and are set free from these bondages."

His voice fades as a small crowd tightens.

"The rock the little among us is climbing is the same one they have launched upon us. It's the same one that you may have to dodge someday. You might climb over it or hide behind it, but its presence and substantial distress are unmistaken and unavoidable. There is nothing new under the sun, I tell you, nothing."

Someone from the crowd shouts, "You tell them, Brother!"

A woman responds, "Yes. Let the truth be told, Brother Dan!"

Coming into view, Raymond's shoes point toward the fast-moving traffic, pauses for a split second, and then turns in the direction of Dan's crate. He is drawn to the words and overtaken by the familiar principles his father once spoke of. He removes his glasses and draws closer to the speaker on the shoeshine crate, decorous and focused. Stitched on Dan's coat is a symbol Raymond remembers seeing in his father's garden as a child. It is translated to mean "In the beginning was the Word, and the Word was with God, and the Word was God." In reality, these words symbolically and collectively point to the essence in the *Book of Wisdom and Salvation*. He was taught at an early age the principle of these words and the power they possess. The Moyennes were very careful to follow the tenet: "Do not create for yourself an image in the form of anything in heaven above or on the earth beneath or in the waters below." They found an exception in the mezuzah. The inscription on his coat resembled the mezuzah hung above his father's garden entrance.

He brushes off his vest, composes his emotions, and continues to listen. Time seems to stand still as a sweet vanilla smell enters his nostrils and reminds him of the calming voice of his mother on the grounds of a small cottage in the country where he would visit his grandparents.

"Raymond, can you find meaning in this, my boy?" She handed him an inscribed horse saddle. His reflection on the collation of his mother's words is soon interrupted by sirens approaching the market square, breaking into the congested streets.

Fleeing horrific conflicts from the countryside, many had migrated to the square and found solace in small movements like the one championed by Dan—a movement that put him in the crosshairs of Folium's ministries. It is unlawful to congregate in the squares like this, and they are faced with a surprise raid. At the eleventh hour, when morning Mass had already ended—and presumed complacency had reached its peak—they make their move.

A loud blast followed by screams of flying smoke canisters deafens the crowd, causing even the protruding rocks from the nearby inclined homes to tremble. The ruckus creates confusion among the escapees as they frantically scatter from the oncoming armored vehicles.

"Stop where ever you are! You will not be harmed!"

Another canister is fired. Some run deeper into the markets, and others who have learned from the past conform to the setting and pretend to be part of the routine traffic. Nevertheless, a few are still captured, but that doesn't sufficiently suit their purpose. The assailing agents are given strict orders to arrest two individuals of interests.

An informant of the ministries provided critical information on Raymond's arrival at the square. It is believed that he plans to meet with members of the Magma in their covert plan to destabilize the ministries. Raymond is known as a fearlessly outspoken objector of the criminal dealings of the ministries and the shadow institutions they shelter. They, therefore, see him as a threat to an established social order.

"We have visual of the target, heading at twelve o'clock and approaching your direction, Team Bravo. Do you read?"

"Affirmative. We have birds heading in. Over."

Speaking into his wristwatch, the commander shouts, "I've tagged the target! He is among friendlies. Do you copy? I repeat. He is under cover of friendlies. Do not fire? Do you copy?"

Raymond realizes the large black vehicle is approaching and runs inside one of the market stands, parting through their hanging beads and ornamental curtains. An agent jumps off the vehicle and chases after Raymond, jumping over a broken alabaster vase and a wooden bench. "Stop that man!" he yells out to the confused patrons. "Out of my way!" The agent ransacks the merchandise. Other agents also go on the pursuit.

Left behind and overlooked, Dan takes off his hat and blends in with the crowd. Shifting his shoulder bag to his other arm, he ducks into a creamery. "Assalamu Alaykum."

The female attendant replies, "Wa Alaykum Assalam."

He orders a mamounia, and she serves him a bowl of sweet pudding sprinkled with walnuts.

"Would you like your cinnamon light or heavy?" she asks. Her children are sitting in the rear of the café, drawing figurines on a chalk tablet. Her husband appears from the back room and brings in a box of freshly cut roses delivered by a young delivery boy in a Pluton shirt.

"My good man, may the Most High bless you and your family," Dan says.

"Ah, you are one of those Christian converts, huh? That's respectable, I suppose. I thank you for the blessing, my brother. Here, take this. It is on the house." He hands him a freshly baked kunafeh with sprinkled pistachio. The creamy dessert is a delicious and crunchy and whets Dan's appetite for more, but he mustn't stay too long. He relaxes his nerves and continues to enjoy the dishes, but he occasionally looks up for any approaching agents.

Still running from the agents and the mercenaries, Raymond sees a flagship at the horizon and decides to cut into a narrow alley. Emerging on the other side, he sees a crowd of youths playing soccer and decides to blend in with them. He removes his jacket and stands beside a short elderly woman hanging wet clothes to dry.

She looks up at him and smiles. "You look familiar, my boy."

Raymond shakes his head, hoping that she would carry on with her chores, but she insists on focusing on him. He stays there for a while, answering her curiosities with nods and shakes, but he can't seem to disinterest the elderly lady. "Madam, you don't know me."

Realizing that he is in a compromising position, he walks quickly between two shanty buildings and an alley. He turns around and catches the attention of the old lady's husband who emerged from the unfinished brick house. Wearing oversized white lapels, brown trousers, and confidently standing in oversized boots, he waves for his attention. He shouts, "My son, where are you going?"

Raymond continues to run until he can no longer hear the old man, but he soon hears gunfire and cars screeching blocks away. He wonders if they are closer than they seem. He stops to listen for the direction of the shooting. He looks to the left and the right and then above the buildings, but he is still uncertain. He begins to run again, but the vehicles are getting even closer. He spreads the lines in his forehead and inhales. "I can do this," he says to himself as he climbs under an abandoned horse cart.

A helicopter crosses over and circles back, hovering over the trees. The operator in the helicopter speaks to the radio, saying, "Target has left the cover of friendlies and is on foot and approaching the Bear Land wall."

Oh my soul. Oh, my soul. Oh my soul. May God above help me! Raymond runs faster and faster, but he feels as though he is running on a wheel and going nowhere fast. Raymond soon realizes that is he is running in a maze.

The town is purposely designed with all exits leading back to the market. Having realized this, he returns from the alley, up to the funnels of the market streets, in search of optimism.

Optimism left the moment he entered the maze. The probability of hope lessened with the hour and left him with only the consequences of courage. This revelation brings him to a decision: to continue to run and be shot in the back or turn himself in to the agents and deal with the consequences. Heavy breathing and whispers blended in his head: *Oh my soul. They are here. The raiders are here! The raiders are here! The raiders are here!*

Everything around him seems to be moving like a fast smear of wet red, yellow, and blue paint, like the paintings sold at one of Folium's shipping ports, abstract works of art created by young scholars he once worked with in his university.

The menacing sounds above merge with the garbled voices throughout the shanties. The spinning imagery and muffled sounds in his head daze him beyond any ability to fight, and as his unrestrained breathing increases, he can only stand still. He comes to a point where his legs begin to fail, and he catches very little air. Forced to stop in front of a cattle-shearing shop, he stoops down to catch his breath. *I think I have lost them.*

A boy flying a green kite on one of the rooftops yells, "*Você precisa executar!*"

Raymond doesn't understand and looks all around him for a connection. The boy yells, "*Corre!*"

Suddenly, Raymond is encircled by the large black vehicles. Three agents step out of the one blocking the only possible escape route. "Come with me," says an agent. The elephantine man towers over the other agents. They wrestle Raymond to the ground and attempt to drag him into the bulky vehicle. Another agent extends his hand from inside and tries to grab him by his collar, but he grabs his jacket instead. Raymond gets a glimpse at his dark glasses and his biometric badge, which reads: "Property of Global Ministries."

"Sir, we are not going to harm you. We simply have a few questions to ask of you." An agent points his ray gun at Raymond. The agent doesn't look like a citizen of the district and speaks with a thick accent. In fact, the team members come from throughout Folium.

Breathing profoundly, Raymond responds, "What do you want with me? I haven't done anything wrong. I have my papers if you want to see them. Am I legally traveling in this district?"

An agent who sounds more like a resident of Bidonville tries to negotiate a peaceful arrest. "Raymond, we all can go home safely tonight if we make this easy. In fact, we all want this to be a smooth and quick process. We just need to scan your chip and ask you a few questions. You will you be on your way."

Raymond extends his right arm as the agents approach. His shoulders rise and drop rapidly as he breathes heavier and heavier. His heart races as they lower their contraption to his arm. An ultra-blue light emits from the muzzle.

In the square, Dan walks out into the street, tucks in his shirt, secures his jacket, and waves down a cab. One of the drivers wearing designer spectacles wipes his sweaty face with a faded green towel. His stubby, ornamented fingers wrestle the wheel to quickly bring the vehicle in Dan's direction before another driver does. A slim woman and her small boy peer into his dusty windshield and ask if he is in service. He flags them away so as to not lose the chance to swiftly get to Dan. "No. Sorry, lady. I am not for hire." He makes his way to in Dan, nearly hitting the mud-stained sidewalk. "Where you are headed, Nobleman?"

Dan replies, "Take me away from here—outside the squares."

"Yes, sir! I will do my best, but this traffic is wild," says the driver.

Dan steps into the cab and takes a seat. He slowly slides his fingers on the smooth wooden trim of the doors, not making eye contact with the driver. "Very well." Dan sits back and pops gum into his mouth.

They move past the colorful storefronts and occasional potholes along the unevenly paved road as traffic permits.

Thirty minutes into the ride, they are a few blocks away from where the raid occurred.

Looking through the bottom of his shades, the driver puts chewing sticks in his mouth. "Are you some sort of an activist or something?"

Dan takes his focus off the pedestrians and quickly looks at the rearview mirror. "Excuse me?"

"Ah, never mind. Hey, do you like debugging music."

"Sure. Whatever you've got." Dan nervously rubs his hands together and stretches his neck.

"You see there?" The driver taps on his windshield like a woodpecker.

Maintaining a motionless form, without moving his head, Dan rolls his eyes in the direction of the stubby fingers.

"Those are some of the nicest dresses in town. My sister is a seamstress and makes plenty of dresses like those, but she cannot find work because the imports have flooded the market. So she resorted to other affairs. I begged her to continue her studies, but she refused. You see, she is in love with that man. I tell you that man is no good for her. Let me tell about the time—"

Dan sighs. "Driver, excuse me again. I mean no disrespect, but I am becoming impatient with this traffic. Has traffic been this maddening today? We have been in traffic over half an hour."

The driver shrugs. "Um … yeah, but you know how things are at this time of the day." The driver chuckles. "It's the middle of the day. What else would you expect?"

It's been quite some time since the raid began, and the people at the market are resuming their shopping and daily affairs. They are like sheep grazing in an open field of grass—as though nothing had just happened a few blocks from where they stand. Raids have become a normal occurrence and no longer draw the same amount of shock and awe they once did. A few attentive people stop to take notice of clusters of people running, but they consider it another day of runaway bandits.

"Stop that bandit," a toothless man shouts from his upper deck window.

No one takes notice. It is just not the sort of thing one finds engaging anymore.

The driver accelerates to close a gap left open by cabs pulling over for passengers and comes to an abrupt stop in front of a jewelry store as a man runs in front of them.

"Raymond!" shouts Dan. "It is Raymond! Come in! Come in!"

Raymond jumps in, managing to escape the agents.

"How did you manage to get away?" He looks at the driver and back at Raymond and says, "How did you find me? We've been driving for hours since you cut through those buildings."

They both look back to see if they are being followed. They sigh in relief that they have evaded the raiders.

"You must have activated your beacon, Raymond," says Dan.

Huffing and puffing, Raymond replies, "Yes. How did you know?"

Dan replies, "Let's just say a lion is recognized by his roar."

Raymond brushes his head with his sweaty hand and says, "I am Raymond Moyenne."

Dan grins. "I know who you are, my brother."

Raymond says, "Let me ask you, my brother, have been to the father's house?"

Dan replies, "Not yet, my brother, but I have my name written inside the resident halls in the great *Book of Life*. I understand there are many dwelling places in our Father's house, and I hope to meet you there someday."

Raymond smiles and shakes Dan's hand. "I was heading for the chalet and Iconium on 14-AC Street. I have an important meeting with remote members of our temple. Would you do me the honor and join me? We can head there together while we still have time."

"Absolutely! Raymond, the great debater. I can't believe it!"

"You can join me as a guest," says Raymond.

"I would be honored," replies Dan.

"Great! Driver, can you change course?" asks Raymond.

The cab makes a slow yield, turns around the stronghold fountain, and stops at the crossing. "Certainly, my good gentlemen. You have been very busy today, I see. Should I wait for you there?"

"No, we will stay the night," replies Raymond.

Raymond looks at the reflection of the cab from the glass of a bookstore and focuses on a prominent display of books: some on the Pool of Siloam, the destruction of the Maleficent, collections of the Apocrypha, and other books on interesting topics.

He reads from the cab's advertisement affixed to the side door—*939*—a measurement in miles to Mosaic Point, Africa."

"Your father," says Dan.

Startled, Raymond responds, "What?"

"Does your father still write books?"

"Oh, yes. Sorry. My mind was somewhere else for a moment," responds Raymond.

The two gentlemen immediately strike up a thought-provoking conversation that settles their angst. The ride, however, leaves much to be desired.

The left-handed taxi driver appears to be anxious in his maneuvers and unsure of his destination. Crossing every intersection as though looking for a lost kitten in the dark, he is preoccupied with every flash of moving color and every vendor call. Moving his bulgy eyes in every direction, he surveys the roads. He pauses and ducks his head below his visor for quick glances at the backseat and back to the road again. There is something odd about this driver, but since he was the only opportune escape, they convince themselves to patiently sit for the ride.

Dan asks, "What made you stop at the market? Were you waiting for your lift there?"

"No, my brother. Actually, I was with the professor. We both took the central bus together to the Iron Bull Market. I was headed to the Marche Noir. I decided to walk a few blocks further. I was going to buy something there, but along the way, I stopped by the Maldives fish market to toss a few coins into a musician's hat. I ran into an old friend who was carrying one of my publications."

"Which one?" Dan asks.

"*Kings of Folium.* It speaks of Folium historic districts, which spans across all the major continental seas and how she had them numbered and controlled with central strongholds. Inside each district are colonies of sub-districts. They all serve their purpose, you see. Ever wondered why our religious, military, and financial ministries all reside in separate districts? Take Bidonville, for example. She is one of four districts Folium is trying to engineer. She's been at it for centuries. This land we call home, while it is not our genesis, is the essence we carry with us now. Wherever I go in the Continuum, if my mind remains with Bidonville, I am she—and she is in me. There are many Bidonville out there, but this district is my home no matter what the Folium system engineers."

Dan replies, "The global Bidonville never has and will never be free as I see it."

Raymond replies, "That is one philosophy, but if it is defeat by starvation they want, I say we snatch Bidonville out from her global system, create our own sustenance, and feed our own people from our God-given land. As we feed our faith, we begin to starve our greatest fears and weaknesses and become a nation like none other: a God-fearing nation capable of doing unimaginable things if we dare."

"What do you mean?" asks Dan.

"It's a crazy idea, but it is crazy enough to work. Bidonville ought to disconnect herself from Folium's monetary system and revert to bartering, both locally and in our exported commodities with sister districts. We can do it. We can create our own economy, an economy of manpower, based on our local strength and trade advantages. We could create a group economy where the fruits of our labor would be permitted, uninhibited to cycle seven times more than that of today. I can see us bringing it to fruition. We can be a genuine republic again—by the people and for the people. It can be done without their dreadful chips!"

"But the world is global, my brother. I don't think you will get very far with such an idea," says Dan.

"Ah, that's just it, my brother. Globalism is another linchpin to the invisible machine. The idea is possible—but not under the current Folium system, you see."

Dan rubs his eyes and takes in a deep breath. "If it gets any hotter in here, were are going to have to walk instead."

Raymond says, "Think of it—a perfect hierarchy based on a new structure: God, family, and then nation. It would be the ultimate utopia district, which we could spread out throughout Folium. I worry that day will never arrive because the people lack the fortitude and foresight. They can't see it because they are already sitting at the king's table, eating their quail meat, and drinking their wine. It's a double-edged sword, surviving in an age of deception and servitude while preserving self-autonomy."

Caressing his chin, Dan replies, "You have an interesting perspective there. This is an interesting point of view, but it is a difficult prospect. Now, what of your faith and lineage? The rest of Folium does not take too kindly a man such as yourself."

"Whatever Folium creates, it can destroy. Don't allow her to define who you are—lest you become lost in her definitions, classifications, and categorizations. She will place value on your life and remove value as she sees fit. While both you and I are predestined from two different lines, we are one family under the Most High, regardless of what we look like or where we live in Continuum."

Dan says, "Ah, yes. The fabrication of a man is the easiest thing to do when he doesn't know himself. I read this in one of your father's publications."

"Now you are talking, my good man," says Raymond.

Raymond takes a glimpse outside his window and says, "It is getting hotter in here."

A large unmarked vehicle crosses their path, heading in the opposite direction.

Raymond says, "Okay, back to the market. We decided to have lunch and then parted. Afterward, I fancied a shoeshine, but that was not to be. In any event, I took notice of a following that encircled a man with a strong constitution and purpose."

They focus their attention outside.

Dan nods and says, "Raymond, is she indeed the land of the mountains or is the book a metaphor of districts that mirrors her contradictions. Her story sounds an awful like the land of the Taino and Arawak."

Raymond chuckles. "My brother, let me put it this way. I will put it the way my father once did for me, but in brevity because we haven't had time to unpack this in such a short cab ride. There was a man who traveled on the rough seas of the two plates that once were one larger plate. After the divide, he lost connection with himself and where he came from. It was not until he bled out the streams of Folium that his true self was revealed to him. I am not talking about paganism. We are against this. I am speaking about the process of coming to know his true identity in the Most High. This required him to shed his old self. The blood that flows through his veins was tinted with the Continuum system. He needed to receive the infusion of the Light to live as a new man destined to his original home, which is not here on this plane, but out there. I say out there and not up there because direction—north, east, west, and south—only apply here on Continuum. We are all souls living hidden to ourselves in dying vessels."

Dan opens his eyes wide. "Those are the words he spoke?"

"Which words and whom do you speak of?" asked Raymond.

Dan says, "The vessel part. Our family migrated from the southern kingdom and served under the direction of the elders. Those were the words I often heard."

"Pardon my overindulgence, but please tell me about your family," Raymond says.

Dan opens his eyes wide. "My father spoke of membership in a devout group that helped protect believers of the faith migrating across the deserts. It's interesting that you would mention this. He often told me that there would come a day when the umbilical cords of twin brothers would be used to strangle their people with falsehood, turning their eyes away from the Most High, a deception of the centuries. Our family came to follow the teachings of the Messianic canons and eventually migrated to Bidonville, where my father served as an elder and counselor. I always wanted to go back to bring truth and light to my people, but my undertaking for the moment has been here."

The market steam lingers in the air and dances with the diesel exhaust in the congested square. The colorful figures of fast-moving arms, crowded feet, and swinging hips move about, careful not to bump into box-toting wheelbarrows and charcoal peddlers trying to find their way to the middle of the square.

Fanning away pesky fruit flies from the sweet drizzles of yellow and orange mangos, star fruit blisters, star apple, quenepes, guavas, and sugarcane stacks, the vendors call to passersby for their interest. The market is bustling and active, inundating their senses with the productivity of the market streets. They remain camouflaged in the vast open space, observing life in a slow-motion cab.

The taxi's bald tires come to an abrupt stop and slowly roll over a foreign coin in a muddy puddle. It must have been dropped by someone traveling from one of the far districts. The partially visible face of the woman on the coin glistens and catches the attention of a man waiting for the cab to move on.

Dan looks out the partially lowered window, surveys the direction of the traffic, and inhales the heavy air, hoping it will quell the anxious butterflies dancing in his stomach.

The driver looks at his watch and sticks his head out the window. "Get out of the way," He honks his horn and twists and turns his wheel to maneuver through the bottleneck as more cars and trucks enter the main street.

Dan says, "Don't you think we would be better off walking from here? We are not getting anywhere in this hot box."

The driver says, "Whose idea was it to give these imbeciles a license to drive? Hey, you pig, don't you see I'm trying to get through?" The driver looks in his rearview mirror. "Gentlemen, hang in there. I know you must be hot and frustrated by now, but I know another way out." He aggressively turns onto a narrow street, passing the butcher and baker, and turns again, nearly knocking over a pistachio and cassava stand. "There! Okay! We'll be out of here in no time, my friends."

Raymond replies, "We are trying to get to the chalet … alive!"

"Yes. Yes. I know. This is the back road. I know where I am going. I know these parts like the back of my hand," says the driver.

The young men agree to the reroute despite their distrust of the driver.

Spinning the radio's broken knob to increase the volume to a staticky reception, the driver adjusts his shades and begins to relax.

On the radio, an announcer interrupts the music. "This is your friend on Valley Top Radio, bringing you live traffic, uninterrupted music, and local news. It's fifteen past the hour. It's a hot and busy day at the square today. Be sure to bring your walking shoes because you are going to need it. The FMF is paying a three-day official visit to Bidonville at this pivotal moment in history. Therefore, expect traffic congestions and protesters."

Music begins to play more clearly, but the announcer soon interrupts it again. "We have reports of heavy congestion on the west side of Loyalist Bridge. You will want to take a detour to the slope and run. Those protesters must be at it again. This song comes to you from the district of Slogtown." Music begins to play again with guitars introducing the voice of a popular singer from Slogtown who formed a band with members from across Folium. "Mama, I want to stay, but I have to go … go … go … to the far … far … far … land of Freedom land." He is exiled now, but his music is beloved by the people.

The driver tries to hum along.

"Others may want to stay there, Mama, but I have to move on for you, Mama. Some say things will be getting better soon someday, but they've been saying that since I was a baby, Mama. Back in my heydays, heydays, heydays, same mind, same thoughts, same habits, same chains, never change … they stay, they stay, stay, they stay … hey … hey … hey … hey! They say, but they stay, they say, and choose to stay, but I've got to move on, Mama."

The driver appears to be detouring from the direction of the hills.

Trying to speak over the loud music, Raymond shouts, "Driver? Driver!"

The driver turns down the radio.

Raymond says, "Driver, sorry to be a nuisance, but Iconium isn't near the ocean. Are you sure this is the way?"

"It's beautiful, isn't? I like to take in these scenic views after a long day of circling the squares. We are getting there soon. Relax!"

The uncomfortable ride bobs the heads of the passengers and slams their backs to the hot leather seat.

Minutes later, the cab leaves the paved roads of the square and enters the obscurity of the countryside.

It is still early part, and participation in commerce and commuting is expected to continue into the night. Traffic congestion is normal and will remain so until dusk. The lazy afternoon of the hills is miles away, and they do not seem to be inviting company anytime soon. They don't expect much fanfare there. They drive past the National Artillery building and stop again for a man and his burdened donkey.

Dan takes hold of the passenger seat and leans forward. "Where are we, driver?" he asks the driver.

The driver replies, "Rats!"

"What's the problem?" Raymond asks.

"I am low on fuel. Hang on. I have to make a stop—and then we will be on our way to Iconium."

Raymond and Dan nervously agree.

While reversing gear, the cab rattles its muffler against a jagged rock inside a rosebush.

"What was that?" asks Raymond.

"They must have put that there last night to block the ministry trucks from entering," says the driver.

"Who's *they*?" asks Raymond

The driver shrugs. "You heard of the Atlas, haven't you?"

They look back at the bush as the cab descends the hill. Still looking back, they both say, "Yes."

"That will tell you what you need to know."

The driver continues for another hour, and Dan says, "Excuse me, driver. Shouldn't we have arrived by now?"

"Yes. Don't worry. Everything will be all right, my friends. We are almost there." He pulls in front of a large iron gate. Its faded red paint pales against the glossy veneer of two Venetian columns. The driver steps out and joins a couple of men smoking pipes. They engage in a conversation and occasionally look back at the cab.

The men seem to know something that the passengers don't know. The suspicious men, who appear to be guardsmen, remove their hands from their pockets and embrace the driver. One of the men waves his index finger and receives a nod from the driver. The other reaches inside a small bag on the floor and hands him a package. He exhales a puff of smoke, holds the driver's shoulders, and seems to explain something to him.

The driver raises his hand and returns to the cab.

Raymond and Dan realize it is no ordinary cab ride. "Driver! I think we should be okay here. What is the fare?" They try to open the doors but are unable to open from the inside.

"Ah, sorry, my friends. They are broken. I have meant to fix them. We are almost there. Oh! By the way, I am going to need to increase your fare because of the detour."

"What?" Dan shouts. "What's going on here? We didn't agree to come here. You had plenty of opportunities in your detours. That was your decision to come here—not ours."

"Dan, wait. Let us be reasonable with this man. We are not in a position to bargain out here in the middle of this town. Let's just pay him and thank God we haven't been killed. I don't like the way those men looked at us back there. Besides, for some reason, he is purposely trying to anger us … perhaps to weaken our concentration for something less trivial."

Dan replies, "Sir, we will pay your fare, but we ask that you let out at the next turn."

"I can't," says the driver.

"What do you mean?" Raymond says.

The driver presses the gas, makes a tight turn down the slope, and heads up another hill. He slightly raises his guayabera shirt to display his weapon. "I suggest you sit back quietly and relax."

The broken radio knob and jammed doors are not the only broken instruments in the car. The gas gauge appears to be too. It has been a ploy all along. They realize they have been kidnaped and are headed to a nefarious location.

Rubbing his legs, Raymond takes in a deep breath. "Dan, we have been kidnaped."

Dan whispers, "Let's kick in the window and get out of here. He is taking us to market like sheep to slaughter. Oh, no! I can't believe they manage to take both of us like this. He knows who we are."

The driver turns onto a hidden path. They drive through an extended private road, hugged by an assortment of beautiful trees and flowers overlooking the roofs of secluded mansions.

Two guards appear out of nowhere and approach the cab. One of the guards looks into the vehicle and speaks into a hidden mic in his jacket. "There are here, sir." He waves them into the large mechanical gates.

"Someone invited us to this party but forgot to tell us about it," Dan says.

Raymond says, "It's going to require a king's ransom to get out of here."

"That's if we are here as kidnapped activists or for something else," Dan replies.

"If our merciful and wonderful God is for us, who can be against us, eh," Raymond says.

"So be it … truly," Dan replies.

One of the guards signals for his trained German shepherd to inspect the vehicle. The driver is told to drive forward. The large dog obediently sniffs the bald tires as it slowly moves onto the Italian pavers. The driver stops and steps out to join more guards. Stepping forward from the side door, a tall, slender man dressed in white and holding a black cane removes his hat. The driver walks toward him and is handed a larger package. They exchange a few words.

As the driver returns to the cab, he stops and follows a dangling line up to a tree. He continues toward the cab. "All right. Sorry, young men. The ride ends here."

The armed guards at the gate escort Raymond and Dan to a side door. The slender man with the cane receives them.

"Good afternoon, Mr. Rome," says a guard. "Our assets have arrived without incident and are ready to be processed."

Mr. Rome adjusts the patch over his right eye and limps past amphora vases depicting the twelve Olympians and back into the entrance, leaving the misty garden and armed guards outside.

CHAPTER
FOURTEEN
•••

The Mansion

High and low ranges of operatic vocals and strings surround the immense grandeur of the hall. It plays at a distance, but echoes of the geometrically shaped walls reach through the drowning sound of the waterfalls.

The water channels from several ports or eyelets behind a glass shield. It is as though the eyes on the walls are crying for the unsuspecting prisoners being led to their demise. Raymond begins to reminisce about his mother's smile and the warm embrace of his father. "Son, you are one significant piece in a game of chess played by men you do not know. This remains true as long as you agree to be played. Remember who you are, never walk away from it, and never agree to be in the council of the ungodly." In his mind, he sees the birds flocking across the sky, drawing invisible lines across the horizon, and speaking to him of God's grandeur. They do not sow, reap, or gather into barns. The Most High cares for them.

Their shadows precede them into the halls, and the casting light alternates between the branches and columns. The music begins to get louder as they walk the procession with guards they cannot see. Their steps follow in unison as they make their way closer to another hall where the violin and piano are amplified. The notes dance a slow dance to the tune of melancholy hues, like the colors painted outside the great cathedral.

Dan whispers, "Take heart, my brother. Today was a great day. We have served well. No matter what happens to us today, it is a gain for Christ. I am honored to have spent these hours with you. You know, I can see an unexpected ending in my mind's eye. I see myself standing in the center of fields and walking in their beauty to the other side where many of my ancestors wait. In the middle of spring, my mother once waited for me to come home, but it is all relative to me now."

Mr. Rome asks, "What have you recovered? Were you able to work your magic and revive the machine after the solar storm?"

A technician says, "Yes, sir. We are recovering full power and should be ready for processing within an hour."

"Very well then. I shall alert the council," says Mr. Rome.

Raymond, Dan, Mr. Rome, and two other guards approach a large elevator that seems to ascend and descend at great heights within the mansion. Outside the large doors, men congregate in groups. Others join them and then leave. It is puzzling to Raymond and Dan. It looks like Grand Central Junction.

"Where are we? Where are these people coming from and headed?" Dan asks.

They are dressed like the agents that surrounded Raymond at the Bear Land Wall. The sound of an approaching elevator echoes from behind the indoor wall fountain and stops. More agents exit dressed in dark business suits holding harp-like devices, but only the strings are golden. Raymond and Dan are puzzled by what they are seeing and begin to tremble.

"It's cold in here," Dan says.

"Yes, the temperature just dropped," Raymond replies.

As they approach the distant composition of the orchestra and the range of a French operaist, the guards blindfold them and bind their hands together. They are led into a room where men wait to enter.

"Ladies and gentlemen of this council and witnesses present, I hereby begin the proceedings. Do you so agree?" asks a baritone voice.

"We do. You may begin."

The orchestra fades to a very low volume and is replaced by murmurs of men and women talking over one another. A loud gavel interrupts them.

The man leading the session says, "It is so noted that the souls before us have no legal representation and are under the jurisdiction of Folio Continuum."

A dignified woman replies, "And how do you know this, Councilman? We cannot assume that they are mere subjects of circumstance and not implanted here to subjugate our family? We will not consume another virus from unadulterated subjects." She steps down from her stand and walks over to Raymond and Dan. "You are from the lost tribes."

Raymond whispers, "Can you smell that?"

"Yes," says Dan. "It smells like hot metal."

"We mean you no harm, gentle giants. You have been bounded only as a safety measure to protect members of the council. I am a queen of a far land that has been summoned to negotiate a proposition with you men. My people are dying from a virus and are in desperate need of life—life that you can give them. Certainly, you have it in your hearts to give life, do you not? From my reports, you have dedicated your life to saving others. I see a parallel here."

She displays images in their minds of generations of family members the men do not recognize, but they feel a close connection. They are taken on a mental flight to an old home with multiple floors. In each room, antique tables and bureaus display black-and-white images of little children, some resembling family members they know today. They are inserted into places and times they have never visited to meet a king and his dynasty.

Raymond tries to regain control over his mind, but the vivid images and sounds are too strong and captivating.

The queen says, "My people have protected these little children and have given so much for their happiness. I ask you today to do the same for us. I know you are capable. Would you lend me your will and bestow upon the peaceful people of Unobtainium an unforgettable gift of life. We have traveled for years, searching for the antidote to our degenerate ailment and found your people as suitable hosts. We would have to collaborate to eradicate this disease and famine. Now why you two? Well, gentlemen, you have in you an algorithm and or as you call it antigens that are resistant to our digenetic condition. All we need from you is one drop—1 percent is all we need to activate the antidotal codes. My people will receive life, and your people will too. Will you join us?"

Raymond decides not to fight against the force. "What is your name?"

"I am Diana, ruler over the climates of Frigid and Torrid," she replies.

Dan is puzzled by the exchange.

"And do you recognize Jehovah as the Most High God?" asks Raymond.

"Let us have this discussion some other time. My time is short, and we must carry on with this business before us."

Raymond asks, "You do know of his Son, Yeshua, as well?"

The queen uneasily responds, "Never mind this talk. I need you to focus on the seriousness of this conversation. You can save your people and my people before the eleventh hour and come to know the power you possess in your veins."

Raymond is overtaken with a mighty strength and begins to pray.

The queen says, "I am sure you are familiar with the Iconium? You are also familiar with a certain little lady there for whom you show much care? Let's say she were to disappear or mysteriously come down with an ailment? I have it in my power to see to it that she is not touched and cared for throughout her days. All I ask is a bit of cooperation from you—not this talk of the person you speak of. You seem to be a reasonable man who would look upon my proposition with great consideration and need not muddy up the waters with nonsensical talk. I can bring about snow in this room and show you your father and those who stand beside him. And you, Dan, I have been with your people as well. I know your true and original name and your family line. I have agents with your father at this very hour. He does not know it yet, but he sleeps among those who wander the night. How much do you love your father—more than life itself? The buried bones of your people cry out beneath our feet, but your people cannot hear them because we have made sure to mute every word." She sniffs the air as she walks around the young men. Her countenance begins to morph. "You have been covered by it. I can smell it all over you. The serum—the essence of the one beyond this house. The one you speak of. I can see it in every energy point. You pathetic, confused progenies. Raymond, do you want to see the light of day again? Dan, you poor boy, do you want to return to your people? Alive?"

Raymond and Dan struggle and squirm in their shackles, grinding their teeth.

"It's getting hotter in here," says Dan.

Raymond responds, "Dan! Submit yourselves therefore to God. Resist the devil, and he will flee from you. We are activating, Dan. We are activating the beacon—or it's activating in us. It's a counteraction to whatever she is igniting. Have faith. The God who lives in us is greater than this evil."

"Silence!" the voice shouts.

With perspiring palms, the young men try to control their nerves.

Exhaling and inhaling whatever air is available, Raymond tightens his fist and expands his elbows to signal Dan.

They both begin to pray silently. "Great and merciful Father, Creator of the multiverse, we come to you in the name of your Son, Yeshua the Messiah."

Others begin to shout from the council bench. "Silence!" Shut up! Stop it!"

They continue, "The Lord is my refuge, and I will make the Most High my dwelling. No harm will overtake me. No disaster will come near my tent."

The queen retreats to the shadows of the room, concealing her weakened and defeated state to hide the effects of their prayer and the power in the name of Yeshua the Messiah.

The timekeeper stands up from his position and stares at them. "What do you propose is the ideal remedy for this situation in which you find yourself? Do you possess the wherewithal to change your circumstance with mere words? Do you think you are above this court and the laws from which it operates—the universal laws that govern your topology, you fool? You know nothing of the laws and claim to exercise its powers. We are the law, the authors, and executioners of the laws." He lets out a sinister laugh. "Do you know who I am and from where I come and my dominance? Answer me! Do you know who I am! The time for recompense has passed."

The head councilman of Folio Continuum orders them to be taken to their cell. Raymond and Dan remain uninterrupted in a cylinder cell. Held in isolation with no food or water for twenty-one days, they lose their orientation of day and night. The hours fade in the dark, cold, metallic cells. Night after night, distant echoes of clattering and knocks and screams keep them awake.

Meanwhile, miles from the hidden mansion, the cab driver steps out of his cab and enters a cathedral, head hung low. The radio in his cab continues to play behind him with the keys still dangling from the ignition switch. He buttons up his collar and adjusts his Jurchen Jin watch on his wrist. It was purchased from an underground market, sold by thieves who seized it from exiles of the East District. Their families were victims of a widespread termination after the conquest of their district. He avoids making direct eye contact with the parishioners, moneychangers, and ministry officials while entering through the stained-glass doors and walks past the shiny floors and freshly painted pews to the confession booth. Occasionally frisking his pockets for something lost, he adjusts his collar and straightens his composure. A priest sits across an opaque glass and waits for his confession. The driver rattles silver coins in his pocket and pulls out a rosary.

At the market, the bustling activity of the day remains uninterrupted and unchanged. The national radios fixed high in the middle of the squares plays local music as merchants and patrons exchange the fruits of their labor. The clear skyline is filled with the brilliance of the afternoon sun. The people of Bidonville go about their days unaware of the double handlings and overtness that work around them every day, hidden and tucked away from plain sight.

Further away, in the shanties of Bidonville, a father slides from under his antique car, wipes the oil from his hands, and turns up his radio to decipher the sudden break in the music. It is interrupted by a long beep, and an announcer introduces a member of the ministry.

"My beloved sons and daughters of Folium, I have something to share with you at this hour. It is of utmost importance. I beg for your attention. Your government loves you, and it takes painstaking steps to protect you and ensure your happiness. But, as of late, we have learned of terrible events that we must bring to your attention. It saddens me to say that your safety is at stake. Last night, spies were captured collaborating with the enemy. We discovered them working with outside enemies in the eastern regions."

His son runs up to him impatiently. "Papa … Papa." The boy tries to contain his enthusiasm. "Look at what I have, Papa."

The father simply waves his hand, never turning around to see what his boy had in his hand. He is stricken by what he hears on the radio.

"A man tossed this to me, Papa, when I was flying my kite. He said I will be the next liberator of Bidonville."

"That's nice, my son," his father replies.

In the hills, Mademoiselle Jolie calls her maid. "There is a delivery here for you. It's from the Caspian."

Jolie comes downstairs and sees a pink envelope by the fruit basket in the center of the kitchen table. In curiosity, she turns it over and reads the name of the addressee. It's from Raymond. She quickly opens the letter and is welcomed to its sweet words on richly scented artisan paper. She carefully unfolds the pages of the letter and begins to read: "Ma Jolie Fleur, the sunshine of my day, tonight I decided to write what my heart could best say on paper that my lips could never utter to you in words. You are the cure for my ailment of love. I run to your heart in my mind for that cure since that is the only safe place to look upon your sparkling brown eyes or hear your soft voice whispering in my ear. From your beautiful lips, I hear you say, 'Raymond Moyenne, I will be your cure.' As I waited for you in the mountains in that familiar garden—the one arranged by your eldest sister—I looked upon an angel as you waited for me on your horse. Perhaps when we ride together again, it will not be in secret or a forbidden engagement—but secured by your hand in marriage. I have received news from my father of threats directed toward the temple and my family by nefarious agents of the ministries. While I am concerned for my safety, I am not troubled much as long as I get to see your face again. If you are reading this letter and you have not yet seen me in the spring, I am most certainly in trouble. Fret not, for my love for you will see me through it. You are Ma Jolie, pure and virtuous. Forever I will remember you—and until the day we meet again, I pray you will do the same."

Like the warm rain of Bidonville falling on the green banana leaves of the tropical mountains, her salty tears trickle upon the papers, rendering the letter illegible.

The maid runs to the kitchen, "Mademoiselle, Mademoiselle Jolie!"

Jolie is holding the damp letter to her heart and crying. "Raymond! Raymond! Raymond!"

A cool breeze carries in a light rain. Pitter-patter strikes the kitchen window. The raindrops are dwindling down Jolie's window, flickering with every strike of thunder in the sky. She sees a pattern in the streaming raindrops. They write the poetic notes of a symphony of love. The scales dominated with an AM that wrestles with the emotions of her heart. The sky is darkened with clouds, and more rain covers her window.

At the hideaway, the secret trials continue for the men. They are powerless and voiceless, symbolizing the invisible and forgotten revolutionary men of Folium. They remain invisible to the multitude living out their busy day—far from their silent prayers and supplications.

Will Raymond and Dan become Folium's liberators or more nationless victims? If justice were to peek into the dark cell to distinguish which side of history to stand on this time, she would not be heard. She is without language or borders and exercises at the hands of her handlers—men and women who raid the streets of every district, whether seen or unseen. As great heralds of Bidonville, they know their work is yet to be done. They know that they are at a decision point.

"Dan!" Raymond shouts from across the cell. "Can you hear me?"

He hears a faint voice respond.

"We either fight and face the possibility of impending death or comply with their demands and live yet another day, but under tyranny. If we give in, we live. We live perhaps—but only for a while as we die in our beds tomorrow as cowards and traitors of the kingdom. If we fight, we fight for life. We fight for the life hereafter. We fight for the right to be kings in our own rights and members of his kingdom. They can take our heartbeats, but they cannot take our minds and spirits. We will stand before death again but as men. Free men of Freeland!"

On the twenty-first evening of captivity, Raymond goes into a deep sleep. His mind comes to a restful state, entering an enclosing amplified sound that drowns out all other sounds—even the silent noise in his head. Like crashing transverse waves against the majestic rocks of Atlantis, it overwhelms his senses. It suddenly becomes calm and warm, filled with light and love. He hears a parametric voice like a distant sound that is heard up close. "Fear not. I am the alpha and the omega. For judgment, I came into this world that those who do not see may see. I have heard your prayers and have sent you a messenger. I will open your eyes to see what is hidden to your blind eyes."

Raymond is led into a circular disc platform, moving clockwise in the direction of progressive numeric figures, seemingly representing years of great harvests. Outside the circle, he hears the roars of the Coliseum, cheering on the entrance of new slaves geared up by a haughty emperor for a gory battle. The vibrating rattle of the restrained lions thunders against the solid walls of the semicircular entrapment. At a safe distance—and protected by sentinels—rugged chariot rods kinetically draw momentum as their bronze blades spin in a rapid cycle as they encircle the pit, menacing the slaves with their inevitable fate.

The disc comes to a slow pause and becomes visible to a narrow light shining from an opening, providing a dimensional insight to what he heard outside. Roman soldiers approach in a tortoise formation, marching with lock shields and creating an impenetrable box. A large man runs before his view of the army and smites them with a giant sword. He grabs his chest, and the platform changes to another scene.

Outside the mansion, from across the four squares, something unusual is happening. As lightning and dark clouds begin to blanket the sky, strange iron birds arrive from the obscurity of the clouds, scorching the simple blue horizon with a fiery red mirage. They seem to play the first and second war drums in a vibrating firmament as they move in quickly. Ripping the thin veil between them and the underlying levels, the impressive display of intimidation stuns the people below into confusion and inaction. Staring upward, many people gaze with curiosity and awe at the strange clouds.

Raymond closes his eyes and implores to see no more, but his optics remain outside his control. He hears a distant voice speaking to the kings of antiquity: "Do this, oh great king, and you will rule forever. You will have the power, and we will bear the responsibility of that power."

And then the disc moves again. His focus on the wheels of the chariots is interrupted by the stampede of horses entering the gates of a rulership, and again he hears the mélange ensemble of men, beasts of war, and clashing of swords.

Through the glaring light, an angry king shouts, "Give them a religion! I care not who or what they worship—as long as it is not the one you call the Most High."

A cheer follows from councilmen and delegates from various nations. Again, the same voice appears: "Do this, oh great king, and you will rule forever. You will have the power, and we will bear the responsibility of that power."

Like the chariot wheels, the platform transitions between events, decrees, and disorders. Raymond soon realizes he is an unwilling observer of time—the past, present, and future. The mental flight fills him with dread and angst. *Who are these kings?*

He hears a booming voice reply: "These are the kings who stand before their master and conspire to raise their throne above the stars of God. Beloved, do not imitate evil but imitate good because their day of judgment is coming soon. Whoever does good is from God. Whoever does evil has not seen God."

The disc makes an abrupt stop. Raymond is awakened by a loud wailing and frantically moves about in his cell. He faintly hears a voice crying out, enraged an agony. It increases to a higher pitch over time.

Several guards run past his cell, and then he hears loud sirens. Boots pound the floor, and agents sweep by. He tries to determine what is going on at the end of the hall, but there is not enough evidence—only the loud distressing sound.

One of the guards says, "Your ruckus is not going to make you any less bound."

In the isolated chamber, Dan's chains tighten around his welted body. He looks at the guards, tightens his fists, and grinds his teeth. "I have never backed away from a fight—and today will be no different."

An ominous voice replies, "The mechanisms used to subdue and subjugate the consciousness of the mind is no simple task, Mr. Dan. You are a willing participant in that endeavor." Dressed in a black leather suit, the man stands up in the torture chamber and approaches Dan. "We have been watching you for many years and have come to know you very well. More so than yourself. What is mind?" He removes his dark glasses, black top hat, and sneakers. "Is it the matter in your head or something much more significant and greater, beyond the confines of this universe? Will it remain the same for you under the duress of fear or the emotion of anger? You see, Mr. Dan, you are in my domain now—in my home. The mind, your mind, is under the confinement of your own weakness. Keep fighting the chains, Mr. Dan. Ha-ha." The sinister laugh overpowers Dan's cries. He makes a piercing scream and whimpers.

Raymond, overcome by a righteous anger, yells, "Close your eyes, Dan! Meditate on the words you have learned. Stop fighting with your body, Dan! Stop! You need to focus your energy on that which is positive. Fight with your mind. The fight is in your mind. Muster your will and fight!"

Dan screeches a few intelligible words. "I ... I ... can't!" Tears stream from his eyes and saturate the sweat induced from his torture. He gasps for air. "Oh soul, my soul, my soul!"

Raymond replies, "The more you fight, the stronger they become. Your anger is being used against you. Meditate, Dan! Keep calling on the name of the Lord and meditate."

"Shut that prisoner up!" the man in the leather suit shouts.

Raymond continues until Dan ceases to struggle and scream.

The next day, Raymond is brought before the council. Seventeen guards transport the Persian cup between the chambers, from the stone room and into the bronze, and then into the iron chamber. In each chamber, he serves the kings of the era a concoction from his cup. Raymond observes as the guard brings the cup before the council. He realizes that this is the same guard responsible for storing the Hemhem crown.

Hefty chains rattle from behind, dragging as though pulling a heavy anchor. Raymond looks up slightly and watches the shadow approach. He looks over and recognizes the man's hands and then continues to look to the man's face. He rejoices to see that Dan has survived.

Still trembling from the torture, he manages to smile. "I don't give up so easily. Thank you, my brother for encouraging me," says Dan.

Both men are led into a large room as the councilmen convene the trial to decide their fate. One of the men begins to speak. He is introduced as the timekeeper.

Raymond recognizes his voice from the court.

"I hereby acknowledge the claims of these persons, by divine institution and universal power of this council, and declare them to be enemies of Folium and her districts. Prisoners Raymond Moyenne the seventh from the Northern Kingdom and Dan of the Nile also known as from the line from the Southern Kingdom are to be taken before the termination vault for execution. You may, at this time, resend your position and take the Folio seal to save your life. How do wish to plea? Accept your implant or die?"

Raymond replies, "Weakness and strength of my body are immaterial. He who lives in us has spoken today."

Encouraged by the stand, Dan joins Raymond. "Long live the Spirit. We cast upon you the fire of the Holy Spirit! Fire, Fire! Fire! Fire!"

"Order … order … order!" The head councilman slams his gavel. "What is your position?"

The men reply, "Long live the Spirit. Holy Spirit fire!"

"We will have none of this! Take them to the cryogenics cell," another member screams, trembling in anger.

The queen leans over to the head councilman and says, "Wait! If it were not for the uniqueness of their deoxyribonucleic code, I would have terminated those beings days ago and not have wasted my time here. Let's be reasonable here. It is because of its ability that I have stepped down here—and for what? You promised sleeping men in the astral form, not awake like these. I need the code, by any means. It is like no other and cannot be reproduced. It must be given to us voluntarily, but bringing them before us fully awake only complicates things. Since you have compromised the plan, we have to employ new measures. According to the laws that govern its regeneration, it cannot be taken by force, but that does not mean I cannot persuade them. My patience is drawing thin. We must obtain the antidote tonight at the eve of the harvest—or we will miss another cycle, thousands of years in your time."

The councilman replies, "Yes, Great One. We have made provisions on the eve of the harvest while the people sleep."

"No, that is not enough!" she replies.

Raymond and Dan shout, "Long live the blameless Holy Spirit … Holy Spirit fire … Holy Spirit Fire!"

The queen stands and shouts, "Don't waste my time! I tried to reason with you, but you have chosen hyponymy over sensibility. Like a child, you are handed words to speak that you do not understand.

You feebleminded fools cannot see what is before you and chant as though your words hold power over me and this court. I can snap and break you into unrecognizable twigs. You have no idea who I am, you little boys. I will devour you sooner or later—as the time draws near. Get them out of here!"

She draws back to the unlit portion of the room, whispering, "We are running out of time. My people have counted on me, and I am failing them. We are running out of time. My cup is empty and must be filled."

One of the guards approaches the men and pushes them to the floor.

"Get your hands off of me." Dan begins to struggle with the guard.

"Get up!" The guard jerks Dan to his feet and leads him behind Raymond.

Both men are filled with distress as they walk down the familiar halls with clattering, knocks, and screams. They come to a closed door where a drilling sound can be heard on the other side of the door. They enter with the guards, are led to a chamber, and are scanned by a large-scale magnetic cylinder machine.

"Their natural algorithm is in sync with the core rods and ready for deactivation," says a technician in a long white lab coat.

"Okay. He is clear, sir," says the technician.

"The orders have been retraced, Sabbatean," says the guard.

They are led to another hall in front of the large elevator. They slowly walk in the hydrogen-filled air.

The mysterious guard walks in behind them and says, "Listen, it's a long boat ride from here. You can either go along with what I tell you or swim with the fishes. You are in the Atlas, traveling at quantum speeds, and must follow my every direction if you are to remain alive. To ensure your safe passage, I must first detach you from your platinum shackles or else you will be burnt alive. Is that understood?"

The men nod.

"Please hold still!"

The elevator doors begin to spiral to a close. While moving up, the circular interior lights dim and the cabin remain in anti-gravitational suspension. They hear a robotic voice from the ceiling and walls. "System translations have an encountered an error. Data integration with host systems has failed. Preparing for core-energy correction. System translations have an encountered an error. Data integration with hosts systems has failed. Preparing for core energy correction."

Raymond and Dan are jolted into a realization that their travels are about to end badly. They look at each other as though sharing the same thought of ambushing the guard.

Raymond firmly plants his feet and holds his breath to begin the attack.

The elevator shoots up at an unimaginable speed, forcing the two to the floor. Their fall is softened by a forceful spread of large wings protruding from the guard's back. Raymond and Dan lose consciousness.

Moments later, they regain awareness and try to adjust their blurry vision.

The guard is standing above them. "Do not be afraid, men. You have seen much and are in shock. I have lowered your pulses to stabilize you for what you have encountered thus far—and for what you are about to experience."

Trying to overcome the demand of numbing extremities and throbbing hearts, they remain frozen in fear and astonishment.

Minutes later, the guard says, "Hold on! We are about to transition. You have been prepared and will survive this crossing."

After regaining full consciousness, they sit up, breathing heavily and weakened by the experience.

The guard looks down at the traumatized young men and says, "Welcome back, men. I am Zeph from the house of Amos. I was sent here to rescue you from your captivity. We have been observing you. It's going to get frigid and dark in here. Listen for my voice. I only have a few minutes to tell you what I am about to say. Listen to me—and listen to me well. The cameras and optical scanners will resume online in fifteen minutes. We have a small window of opportunity before they learn you are off the grid." He enters a series of codes on a holographic panel and pulls out a scanning device.

Blinking their eyes, they crawl in an attempt to stand. Holding onto the embossed straps dangling in the cabin, they bring themselves to an upright position.

"This is wonderful! Your programming code has not been compromised," says Zeph.

As the scanner waves over their bodies, they can see active dots of cryptograms rapidly streaming across the four-dimensional screen.

"I needed to be sure you weren't chipped! Had you accepted and complied, this mission would have been aborted—and you would have been absorbed into the Folium machine. I am pleased that you kept your oath. Here, take these. They are folate tabulates to equalize your GO levels."

Raymond and Dan consume the folate infusions. Suddenly, they experience g-force in with the elevator's rapid ascent. They watch as flashing numbers of each floor pass them by. Raymond and Dan look at each other with astonishment. The display fills the room.

Dan asks, "What is going on?"

Zeph replies, "We are scanning your code for virus agents and validating your beacon logs. You are still part of the conscious network and need to be recognized by the binary navigator." Zeph speaks to an unseen voice in the panel. "Controls, I have an affirmative pass on two units with GOs at 0000459 and nucleobase levels at optimum levels with no AI interfaces. We are at level seven—no negatives, fully charged, and prepared to pass entry to the Shekinah. Over!"

Raymond asks, "Where are you taking us?"

Zeph takes his eyes off the scanner and slowly looks up to Raymond. "When you entered the mansion, you crossed over."

Raymond rubs the back of his head. "What do you mean?"

Zeph asks, "Do you remember the waterfall and the men congregated around it?"

Raymond answers, "Yes—from the moment we were led in."

"From that very moment, you left this quantum reality and entered another dimension. Do you remember the music in the long halls?"

"Yes, it seemed to drown out my thoughts." Dan presses his fingers against his ears.

"It was laced with silent agents," explains Zeph.

Levels after levels on each floor, numbers flashes by—3, 4, 5, 6, 7—and then a sudden halt. Zeph briefly returns to the panel to enter a series of passcodes.

"Wait a minute … the opera music?" asks Raymond.

Zeph looks down at the panel. "No. The other music was playing at Folium's frequency. Perhaps you couldn't hear it because you were three levels deep."

"All we heard was opera music. That is all," says Dan.

Zeph looks up again. "You were in REM."

Raymond says, "What are you saying? Do you mean to say that the music put us asleep? How? I don't remember being sedated. Is it possible for both of us to share the same dream?"

Zeph replies, "It has nothing to do with the music per se. It never does. They would have played whatever their captives or the people of Folium are inclined to listen to. From there, they injected the frequencies and laced it to reprogram their code. You were hit on all fronts, at every level, but it was ineffective. The nuclei chip was just an activator of the embedded code already implanted on the day you were born. They aimed to control the chip in stages, but they needed to dim your beacon first. Fortunately, that chip was deactivated the moment you changed masters and came to the Light. It neutralized the atomic impulses. The eve of the harvest was another part of the atomic charge sent out in waves through this frequency. You were targeted because your code was damaging the entire program. There are many like you in Folium, but you have been chosen for the next cycle. Everything will be explained to you soon. Do not worry, my brothers. You have been faithful servants of the Most High—and you kept your oath."

A control operator speaks through the device held by Zeph. "Okay. Please be on standby. We are almost ready to dock. Zeph, I have two processing units in sight and have authenticated their sequence. Waiting for a leveled equator line for a timely dock at T-minus five, four, three, two, go!"

Dan says, "What's going on? I don't get what you are telling me. I know about Folium and its hydrogenous elements, but what you are telling me is really beyond that scope."

"When you came here to Folium, what did you own?" Zeph asks.

"What do you mean? My family has always worked in the—"

"No, that is not what I mean. When you were born, what did you own?"

"I suppose nothing," replies Raymond.

Zeph replies, "You owned your mind, and that is it. You own it until you decide to render it under the custody of some other entity, such as those who claim the minds in Folium. Think about it, men. All of your possessions are earthbound. Isn't this so? Therefore, what is the point of it all—to accumulate things in this dimension? Isn't it just vanity that you toil in Folium's busy farms to accumulate an evasive illusion? This is not to say you must not work, for this is one of the universal laws, but it must not consume your purpose, your mind, and your essence. Listen, there are those who own the very land you live on and your towns, the districts, all of them, and even Folium. Then there are those who remain hidden that possess this very planet you call home and others like it. The malevolent one who tried to invade your bio codes at the trial should have given you a glimpse into what I am telling you, but as I said earlier, you were in REM."

Dan takes in a deep nervous breath. "All along, my faith was just that: faith. Belief in what I could not see. I didn't know that there is so much we don't know."

Ray says, "Nothing in our books prepared me for this inter-dimensional rescue, waterfalls, opera music, or whatever else we went through. This is too much to take in."

"You are living in a cultivated farm, but you already know this. Some call her a prison planet where you are no more than a fuse powering the great machine, and you already have studied this. The Creator is still in control, regardless, and has rendered power and dominion to servants like you." Zeph toggles the bio panel and displays it to Raymond and Dan. "What you are looking at, gentlemen, is a series of bio codes in REM mode, activated with frequencies emitting from the natural poles of this planet. These cryptograms represent the countless lives in Folium under a hypnotic trance, if you will, living their daily lives, unaware that they are in fact asleep. If you look closer, you will see what is called the God code, the Genesis code that they are trying to compromise and reverse engineer. Some of the families who own the cluster farms or districts have branded their subjects with dermo-code-bearing access keys for the nano agents. Once the subjects reach alpha state, they are uploaded with a series of rapid flashes of light. The false light."

Dan asks, "Let me see if I understand you correctly. You mean to tell me that they tattooed agents into the people?"

Zeph replies, "It goes deeper than that. You have only tapped the surface, gentlemen. They are following the universal laws that rule Folium. Here, take these. They are your bio codes. They were taken away from you in captivity. As you already know, they contain the antidote that has kept you alive this long. It's the beacon from the kingdom that sent me here to rescue you." Zeph inserts coordinates. "I don't have much more time to explain. There is so much more to dive into. When we exit the seventh floor, there will be another man waiting there. He knows of the plan, but I need you to comply with him as if you know nothing about our revelation because there still might be spies on the seas. Our captain is waiting for you and knows who you are. We made arrangements to switch the ships once we set out a few miles from the coast. You will know it when you get there. It's called the *Mosaic*. It will take you to your destination."

Raymond thinks, *The Most High, he who is not bound by time or dimensions, has seen my past, my present, and my future. Into his hand, I surrender.*

Dan says, "When we awake on the other side of time, I hope we are found to be worthy."

"I pray that we are, Dan. I pray that we are," Raymond replies.

Zeph looks up to the rising sun as it cast its light upon the stealth hybrid craft and raises his hand. "Men of Freeland, exiles of Folium, repeat after me. Father, in the name of Jesus, the author, and finisher of my faith, I arise to establish my legal right and dominion over this region and over every territory in which you have given me jurisdictional authority. I submit myself to be kings of this land." He firmly puts his hands on their shoulders and says, "The force of the Eternal is with you. The revolution lives on with you. You have been graced with a new title: kings of Bidonville!"

At that moment, Raymond remembers what his father once told him as a child. "Son, if you want to know if your eyes are opened and that you are not in fact in a deep sleep, an illusion of some sort, do this. When you open the *Book of Wisdom and Salvation*, and this passage is missing, you are asleep." Raymond looks back to Zeph and asks, "Sir, what we must do to be saved?"

Zeph smiles and casts an image of the *Book of Wisdom and Salvation* in the air.

Raymond frantically slides his fingers through the book in search of the answer he seeks.

As he desperately glides his fingers through the holographic pages, the gentle sky erupts with lightning and a dismal storm covers the metal dock and the ship.

Zeph says, "You must go quickly. The time is passing."

Raymond ends his search and runs to join Dan. The two proceed forward until they are no longer visible to Zeph. The *Book of Wisdom and Salvation*, however, remains on an open carousel, displaying on a spinning rotation. An array of passages presents, stops for a few seconds, and rotates again—time after time and half a time.

CHAPTER
FIFTEEN
•••

Are You Awake?

Far away in the middle of the square inside a humble temple, a chant is led by a young elder, "Elohim, the magnificent God and great protector. Elohim … Elohim … Elohim … Elohim!"

Questions remain for the two men: Are they in a shared deep sleep, an illusion, or an anesthetized state to an impending event that their natural minds would not be able to deal with otherwise? Is it to this end that their life mission dies—a mission to liberate and enlighten the enslaved people of Folium and mend the broken covenants? Is this the end of their spiritual quest? What about the fate of Folium and the beloved Bidonville? In a sudden rumble, and not a moment too soon, they hear a booming voice in their minds. The voice is mightier than the thunder of great waters. "Welcome, kingdom men. Today is the first day of your life."

Zeph returns to the seat of the mansion to contend with the Folio Continuum. It is seen from space as an accelerated ball of fire.

From within the mansion's portal rooms, one of the technicians says, "We have ultraviolet angles of rays cascading toward the stratosphere at ninety degrees, and they are generating a massive amount of radiation."

Nicea, another technician, asks, "What are the coordinates?" He notices a green leaf on the floor where the prisoners were processed earlier and says, "How in the world did a leaf get in here?"

All of a sudden, alarms begin to sound.

The second technician shouts, "Fire! Fire! Fire! We are under fire!"

They hear a large explosion miles away from the square. Bidonville' s ocean floor begins to shake with a great quake, creating a boiling disturbance in the depths of the ocean floor and plates. The surface overflows onto the gleaming pillars of the square and beneath the bedrock of the National Cathedral and other sacred sites. It widens secretly and silently, spreading indiscriminately between impoverished and wealthy towns alike, circuitously maneuvering from Atlantis to the western part of the land, unbeknownst to the busy people. Within the concealed calm, a quail traveling from Atlantis lands on a large rock on the coastline. It chirps into the wind as though with an urgent message, warning the sleeping people of impending danger. It chirps and chirps and then flies into the wind.

A commanding, sinister voice overtakes the mansion's sound system, putting everyone at attention. "I dare him to war with this house, this blind and muted fool. At the end of this battle, the outer worlds will learn who the real king of Bidonville is and who the blind one is—the one that wanders Continuum in a maddening course. They will see for themselves who reigns supreme. At the end of this battle, they will see a mute and powerless foe returning to his kingdom for all to see—as a defeated enemy who dared challenge the established order of Folium. Send out the dragon and the king's men to show him the powers of this kingdom!"

The agent says, "Send them the beast! Unleash the beast!"

Zeph is intercepted at the line of the equator and led to a combative realm where an epic confrontation begins between two mighty forces capable of surpassing the feats of nature. Unseen by natural eyes, it transcends the sensitivity of the awakened mind. The combat begins between Zeph and several agents from the house of the Olympians on a quantum battlefield.

Like heat-seeking projectiles, one agent after another is summoned and sent out to intercept the incoming light, heralding atomic powers. "This house will not stand. From the embedded foundations of its evil base to the pillars of its conquered souls, I rain down fire! Tonight, judgment has come for you and your city of perversion!"

The first strike comes from the initial brigade of the Olympians, the primary line of the seven levels of defense. They engage the fight after binding the four corners of Bidonville in an attempt to control the natural elements of the battlefield. Behind them, spear-like objects streak through the skies. The hellfire rips open the clouds, fusing the invisible grids of Folium to a solid blanket, changing the formations and windward direction of the clouds and the frequency of wavelengths in the atmosphere and mesosphere.

A bombardment of energy emits in a rapid sequence to overpower Zeph. He responds with another proclamation, saying, "Who can fight the messenger of the Lord, the Light of righteousness. He strikes down several hundred agents.

An agent blocks the light from the sun, sending many in Bidonville into a subtle panic, but they are soon relieved as the light returns. After moments of struggle, blinding combustion forms around them, masking the identity of the regiments and their weapons of choice.

Moments later, the fight descends to one of the hidden mountains. An emerging army attempts to capture sojourners who are lifting their hands in prayer, but the army is unable to penetrate the fiery barrier formed by the elders.

The leaders shout, "Break the chains—every chain!" They cast invisible chains into the open air to subdue the camp. "Holy Spirit fire. Holy Spirit fire. Holy Spirit fire!"

Link after gravitating link falls upon them, but they are quickly decimated into metal clips raining down on trees, rivers, and the Purkinje Bridge.

"Who will you and your household worship?"

The people reply, "We will worship the Lord, the true God, the Most High, and the Great I Am. Jehovah!" They continue the prayer even though they cannot see the oppression that grips them.

More and more chains are cast out again, but they are ineffective. More agents on bulls crawl out of the caves to fight the praying men and women, but they are incapable of defeating the mountain as an established authority is countering their weapons. The fight continues for hours: on one side, evil and on the other righteousness.

At the eleventh hour, fragments from the mountain come crashing down on the fighting army and presumably on Zeph's head, creating a large plume of dust. A deathly silence comes over Bidonville and the square. A small boy stands next to a fountain and begins to pray.

His mother smiles, moves a black and brown sack to her other shoulder, and stoops down to her son. "Darling, why are you praying?"

He replies, "Father always said whenever a bell chimes, an angel has earned its wings."

She smiles and rubs his head.

Miles away, at the mountain, the rubble begins to move as the ground begins to quake. From the ashes of the struggle and the uncertainty of the outcome, Zeph arises. He stands and ascends into the air. He and several other agents of light lock their wings together and sling down toward Atlantis, plunging to the inmost depths of the ocean at speeds that part the reefs. They arrive at the gates of a large city surrounded by a standing army and their queen.

Above the water, little evidence of the battle and the degree to which its effects have altered the dimensional planes is evident. The legions of agents, their assigned terrestrial kings, their inter-terrestrial queen, the rest of the marine kingdom, and creatures from the deep face the agents of righteousness for a battle of biblical proportions.

The brief tremor temporarily impairs the city lights and causes sanctuaries such as the Iconium to experience a blackout. Inside the sanctuary, behind a praying room, a conversation between two men can be heard behind a closed door.

Someone runs into the prayer room and shouts, "Mr. Moyenne! Are you okay? Are you awake?"

A voice from the darkened room responds, "Yes … yes." He brushes off his clothes and stands. "I was in the middle of prayer, breaking strongholds and commanding God's will upon our city. I am very well, gentlemen. Very well indeed."

A sparkle—a timely flicker of light from a kerosene lamp—brightens the room, but it is unclear to a curious mind who was actually praying in the prayer closet. Was it Raymond or his father, Reimonde? The fact remains, however, that faith is a factor this time.

At the square the following morning, the national cathedral's golden bell tolls three times, piercing the open sky as the sun rises.

The congregation chants, "We live only once, but you live forever. The alpha and the omega, Jehovah! Elohim … Elohim … Elohim!"

Printed in the United States
By Bookmasters